Little Lives

By John Howland Spyker

Little Lives

By John Howland Spyker

78

Fred Jordan Books/*Grosset & Dunlap*/*New York*

For The "Maid of Cadiz":
The Loss Remains . . .

Little Lives

By John Howland Spyker

About the County

* *
*

Washington County, New York, is bordered on the East by the Green Mountains of Southern Vermont, on the North by Lake George, on the West by the Hudson River and the Champlain Barge Canal, and on the South by the Counties of Saratoga, Albany, and Rensselaer.

The landscape is essentially hilly, with some valleys, and the land is now scarcely populated because of the rocky terrain and long winters, but the County is still an important dairying center, being among the dairying sheds for New York, New York, and Boston, and equidistant to both.

The County has one of the lowest per capita incomes in New York (and the Nation); it is settled largely by the descendants of Dutch, Canuck, and Scotch Irish yeomen and farmers, with more recent sprinklings and ejaculations from other minorities, such as the Eyties.

The County seats are in Salem and Hudson Falls; but no town in the County has 10,000 in population.

It is architecturally one of the most beautiful museums of Federal and Victorian houses in New York—particularly the villages of Cambridge, Coila, Greenwich, and Salem.

It was the birthplace of nobody lasting or famous

beyond its borders that I know of, aside from Ethan Allen (and people think he was a Vermonter), and Grandma Moses, but many have been born and died here, or passed on through to go elsewhere; and it is this landscape that gave me suck after I was born here, and in its hot summers and warm autumns I was mothered, and grew to manhood, here, presumably, to die, as well.

John Spyker
Fort Edward,
New York
November 1, 1977

"Discoursed about Universal Character, about Preadmits and of Creation. About insects. I mentioned all vegetables to be females. I told Wild and Aubrey of flying. Wild cold. Drank port."
The Diary of Robert Hooke (1672–1680)

Mrs. Freelove Herrison
* *
*

Her name seems like the contradiction I have always
pondered. Around the time of the War Between the
States she lived in Brownsville, between Bacon Hill
and Gansevoort, New York. I have never seen a picture of Freelove, but I imagine her chin first, and only
then a bosom, prominent, on a long slim bony body.
What was the color of her hair? Perhaps straw, all
greyed down. In those days there were only about
thirty families in Bacon Hill; two baseball teams com-
peted regularly. There was a church, a school, a cobbler, a store, in a little grove. Hard to imagine
Freelove living up to her name among the Hurds and
Van Der Werkers. Blind Man Hindman, a neighbor,
carried two canes, one for walking, and one for Sundays. Freelove made candles out of tallow she had
rendered; and went as a child to the Brownsville
schoolhouse where she wrote with a slate pencil on a
slate board, and never once sat at the head of the
class.

What things unsettled or composed this life consisted, we are told, of Sunday School, Prayer Meet-
ings, Picnics, Spelling Matches, Funeral Services,
Apple Parings, Quilting Parties, Kitchen Dances, and
Donations for the Ministers, but the regularity or
frequency of these events is unclear in the records

available to me. A local chronicler tells us simply they were "a rugged jolly lot of people," these descendants of Johnathan Brown, all relatives.

"Of the social graces little was left to the imagination," writes a certain Bascomb Roberts. "Their life in time was desire modified by customs, as if accoutred to being a whole lifetime."

All abstractions are, finally, coy: Freelove probably had a rag mat over her cellar door she had made herself, and a nice vegetable garden. She dried flowers and wove some cloth. Her husband seems to have been unremarkable; chroniclers do not even record his name. She was a householder, as well as a housekeeper. Behind the large frame Empire Hotel was a slaughterhouse with a high picket fence much frequented by the neighbor boys for pranks; Freelove purchased her fresh meat there.

She may have gone to balls at the Gansevoort Mansion.

She was probably buried after a service at the Brownsville schoolhouse.

She must have known Peter Shearer, who served in the war, was made a prisoner in one of the large Confederate prisons, and came home to Brownsville to live in a dugout made out of a hollow stump in the woods, emerging only at night to find food.

Peter Shearer was a deserter; during the day his dugout was covered with a heavy carpet of ground pine.

Shearer eventually hid under his own house another whole winter. When the government agents caught up with him, at last, the war was about over and he was never reprimanded.

Peter Shearer's big stump rotted away some years

ago, but there are some alive who can still show you where it was.

Those days were probably gentler, if you happened to be at all odd: some people arranged the furniture of their houses at catty-corners, and the Man from Moreau, also known as The Prophet, liked to stop wayfarers and recite from Amos, but afterwards he would give them a hand-whittled walking stick.

In 1848, a neighbor of Zebolin Mott paid 30¢ for a "bamboo hat" to be protected from the sun. This consisted of the matting from a packet of tea made into a brim surrounding a cloth crown. It was recorded as "wonderful."

Calfskin boots cost a dollar for the making, provided you brought the cobbler a calf skin.

Eels were shipped from Montreal to New York City on the canal for the Italian laborers every fall.

One had distant kin in distant places like Snide River, Guilderland, and New Baltimore, but Sandy Hill, just across the other side of the Hudson, was considered a day's "excursion."

A Gansevoort relative of the author Herman Melville, distinguished writer of *Typee* and *Omoo*, made "molasses cakes" for the church picnic, and it was said of this Miss Augusta that she was "very 'close' in demanding all have a piece of this 'simple and plain' confection, or else she did not understand 'sweet-tooth' craving of youth."

The Dutch Reformed Church was constructed of brick; it had thick walls and deep-set windows. A

15

heavily wainscotted basement. The mahogany cap pews were a gift of Herman Gansevoort.

Most accounts by my contemporaries of Freelove's era are either reverential, or cynical. They sentimentalize, or else they reject. I am pretty nearly an outlander, more ignorant than some, struck more by bits of detail than the total sepia haze of the picture: by odd names or locutions, specific items and photographs that have survived, the price paid for caring then, or for this or that piece of merchandise, the naming of obscure regions, dorps, collections of hills, and ponds.

A Miss Fredenburgh taught a select school in the basement of the Reformed Church about 1871.

Niskayuna Joe stropped razors and ground knives and sickles; he was said to be part Algonquin.

Gypsies often camped in the woods in the vicinity of the Charles D. Hurd home, and they traded Indian baskets with the boys for salt pork.

Fort Edward brewed its own beer.

Slaves were kept as late as 1807, and possibly later; and, even that late, one did not go through the nearby forest alone—for "fear of Indians."

There were over thirty doctors in the region, and none of them were specialists.

A popular legend sprang up about a New York hoodlum named Big Mose, over eight feet tall, who could lift horse trolleys on his shoulders with the people still inside them, and swim around Manhattan Island in six or eight strokes; New York was six days away by horse coach.

Very few Bacon Hill people ever journeyed as far as New York City for business, or pleasure. They went to Troy, to Albany, to Pittsfield, and Schenectady, and Saratoga; and, when the area was later interconnected by trolleys, to Glens Falls, Lake George, Warrensburg, and Schroon and Loon Lakes as well.

Freelove Herrison may have had a woman friend named Arilla. When she was permitted to write with ink she may have done the household accounts with a goose-quill pen.

She was descended from Johnathan Brown, who settled the community at Bacon Hill, and she had cousins named Mary Louise and Annette. I can find nothing about her husband, or children, or if, indeed, she had lovers. She owned a house and land, and, at cousin Abner Brown's store, liquor from Troy was sold at 3¢ the glass.

Malechi Martin

* *
*

This pioneering minister of the Methodist persuasion from Bacon Hill also operated a carpentry shop. He was noted for his thunderous sermons, and his equally thunderous singing voice. Malechi Martin sang when he worked at carpentry as well as when he prayed. He had one son who perished with the Grand Army of the Republic in 1863.

Having some acquaintance with the law, Reverend Malechi Martin was also empowered to perform the county's first divorce in 1860. A Grangerville couple had come to him to be married and he performed the ceremony. A year later they returned most unhappy with each other and asked to be severed. Although dubious of his secular authority, Malechi Martin had them stand back to back outside his church beneath a large horse-chestnut tree. Martin asked, "Do you both agree to not turn around and both go straight and never come back?"

"Yes."

"All right, now start; and you are both unmarried from this minute on."

The woman, who was facing west, went on as far as Buffalo and never returned to the County.

Malechi Martin was a great dark bearded man with a prominent brow. He emigrated from Yorkshire in England in 1842, and was called The Gypsy, for his darkness, and that curly black beard. He was a noble swearer, and a prodigious worker. Some recall his sermons could be heard as far as a quarter of a mile from the church door when he chose to preach outside on its steps, but they add his voice was of "uncommon sweetness" and "distinctive and of clear intonation." He sermonized against God and the Devil in all their temporal manifestations and secular forms and particularities, being above all else a believer in the Ministry of Man on Earth, and in the Republic for which we all, to this day, stand.

Malechi Martin's favorite hymn was "I'm Glad Salvation's Free," and his favorite pastoral reading was from *The Life of Cobbet*. He was many times accused of being a fornicator and an adulterer, but this was never proved.

As Fanny Pack Mecklin has recalled: "He would probably be called an old-time Methodist exhorter. . . . Sometimes at Sunday breakfast we could hear his voice though we were a good quarter of a mile from the church as he preached his earthly gospel to the assembled."

For a while Malechi Martin also operated a glove factory and a factory for the making of beaver hats with his brother Gabriel near Grangerville, but they were unsuccessful, and he died beloved by nearly all, a preacher. On his tomb is written:

"His toils are past; his work is done;
  and he is truly blest;
  He fought the fight, the victory won,
  and enters into rest."

When the stone was broken into pieces some years ago by neighboring vandals, a daughter came from

Chittenango and had it reassembled, along with the full text of Hood's account of the French and Indian raid on Fort Ti in 1775.

Among the monuments to Malechi Martin's hard labor and thrift are a smoke house composed almost entirely of the hoof bones of dead cattle, and a chimney stack in the fields near Northumberland to which local people to this day attach much signficance, as it abuts the Champlain Canal, built in 1822, which diverted much traffic from Bacon Hill. He was related by marriage to Vanderwerkers, Kahns, and Disons. Among the various other trades he pursued was as a preacher, a tanner, apple grower, cider presser, and an eel merchant, along with those I have already mentioned; and when he died his body was placed under the big horse-chestnut tree in the front yard of the church, and people gathered from every corner of Washington and Eastern Saratoga County to hear the service.

Also extant is a fragment (extract) of a sermon he delivered to the people of Moreau (named after one of Lafayette's lieutenants) on Shrove Tuesday, 1859, on the subject of God's debt to man.

"He that made us all whole owes us nought," Malechi Martin declared, "save that we can be bent and duty bound to observe his earthly passion and follow not in his ways. God lives in our hearts, not on our shoulders. It is for man to know his God as he knows toil, or the sweet voice of the wind. I pray you all to work, and pray."

In his later years, Malechi Martin was often despondent over the death of his son during the revolt and he had the body brought back to Bacon Hill for reinterment shortly before his own death.

"On Bacon Hill"

Bacon Hill is a pleasant place
With its pretty church and school,
A store to buy your tobacco
And a shop to shoe your mule. . . .

Alexander Baucis
* *
*

According to a local historian, the first telephone in
the County was installed in the home of Alexander
Baucis when he was elected State Senator in 1882,
after serving as assemblyman. This was a great
event.

In 1884, Dr. Moore—son of John Moore, who
penned the lines "On Bacon Hill" above, and also
many more—after studying in the leading hospitals
of Germany and Austria settled in Bacon Hill to practice medicine, and took over the telephone upon
Baucis' death, until he moved to Saratoga and that one
phone became the property of Mr. W. S. Deyoe.

Now I find this a little odd: only one phone meant
he had nobody to speak to unless he called the Falls, or
Saratoga, I suppose. Probably would have done as
well with an earcup and a megaphone, under the circumstances, or—*what???*—a dixie and a piece of
string?

They say many of the well-to-do local boys bought
their way out of the Grand Army of the Republic two
decades earlier.

Also that the Deyoes (an odd-sounding name, I still believe) occupied the handsome Pearsall house in Bacon Hill until it burned down during the flu epidemic of 1917.

They say the first bicycle in Bacon Hill made its appearance as the property of George Van Der Werker who used to ride it to church on Sundays, and that Assemblyman Deyoe around 1890 had telephone lines connected from his plaster mill in Grangerville to the Pearsall house, as did Sheriff Deyoe, or another kinsman, up the back road from Schuylerville. . . .

(Pie à la mode was invented in Cambridge, New York, not too far away.)

It is a fact that rural free delivery through the area was the untiring work of A. G. Deyoe, and our concrete road came about because of untiring effort by Earl Rugg. But who was he?

The first family in the County I know of to install flush toilets were the Romans. When they backed up they later left the County, whereupon others followed suit with considerably more aplomb.

Fidelity Hasbroek

* *
*

The name sounds like a financial institution which Fidelity was assuredly not: she was a pauper, inhabited the workhouse in South Argyle for a while with Pussy Vanderkirk, Biddy Onderdonk, and Lally Greenpaw, all spinsters. She was very old by then, well over one hundred when she died. Younger, she lived with her father on his farm along the Vaughn Road.

Winny Hasbroek was part Welsh on his mother's side; his father had been a lead miner near Pottersville. There were drinkers on both sides of the family, and Fidelity—like the protagonist of Zola's *La Bête Humaine*—seemed to inherit the malaise. "Drunk as Winny Hasbroek's daughter" and "Fidelity the Sot" were common expressions for extraordinary inebriation from Salem to South Argyle, among the farmers and mill hands. Once, at the inn in Battenville, it was reported Fidelity and her best friend Jane Cooper (sometimes called Barrel Jane) "together drank a vat of applejack as wide as a Vermont cheese and two feet deep, on a dare." Nobody has ever recorded exactly how the dare was enunciated. Nor who else was involved. We know only that they were bundled, or lashed, onto both sides of a large Percheron Stallion afterwards and led home by a wagoner named Perryvale.

Fidelity was not fat. She was lean and pretty "with corn-colored hair and wicked blue eyes like bottle glass." She never married, but had one child, "born with a harelip," who died when she was less than a year old. No record of the child's name exists, and there is no existing gravesite. All else that we know of Fidelity comes from a longish letter in her hand and with her signature extant in the Public Library.

"You are probably not aware that, for the longest time, I have found you of some interest. Sir my reputation comes before me wherever I go and it is not the custom in these parts for a gentlewoman to be forward toward the males of the species, but I am not as they say I am, believe me.

"When I was very little I knew of you through my father and his friends, and, once, in the Falls, on a day of the marketing, I was fortunate enough to gaze upon your fair and comely countenance without your noticing me. I was almost struck dumb with the delight. Yes, sir, I do like to sport and drink, but not without descrimination, and I have love enough for you, and more, but am discerning.

"Court me. Come to me at the next full moon. Take me out in your rick for a drive among the newly mown fields and I shall moan in your arms until it is dawn. I am yours, forever, if you should want me, and, if not, there shall always be others. . . .

                                        Fidelity."

She wrote in a small hand with brown ink on something that we would now call tissue paper but which has long since turned brownish with age, like butcher paper.

The letter is not addressed; we don't even know if it was ever sent. There's a lock, or twist, of faded yellowish-brown hair, as stiff now as cat whiskers, in the same packet, and a few dry shreds of purple crocus. There's also a photograph (made in Berlin, New York, according to the legend on its backing) of a very young, female child, in a christening gown, reclining against what appears to be a velvet pillow supported by two large masculine hands which have been cut off at the wrists.

The child's eyes are closed. It is not awfully clear if she is alive or dead.

A very fat woman with pigtails in the Crandall Library collection has been identified for me as Barrel Jane, and I have also seen a photograph in sepias of a muddy brown road, a fence, a shack, a grazing grey nag, said to be the homestead of Winny Hasbroek.

Edna Ball

*
  *
   *

She ran off with another man, they always say of Edna
Ball. Never say who.

The affair was scandalous one hundred years ago,
but now it seems just another way of reminding the
descendants of Edna Ball that they hail from tainted
blood.

Edna Ball was a capable woman, people add. The
house was in her name. She worked in the Saratoga
Creamery. Her husband—was his name Abner or
Eben?—had a way of wandering off. He was bad
about paying bills and things.

The Balls owned two houses in Fort Edward, and a
large farm outside Gansevoort. They rented the farm
to some people from Albany, Italians new to the area,
and they moved a sister and her children into the
adjacent house, and went about their business.
Abner, or Eben, had many professions: farmer,
baker, herb doctor, blacksmith, he retired young and
spent most of his last twenty years on earth visiting
his children, once Edna had run away.

"We always liked to have Grandpa staying over,"
a granddaughter recalls. "He told us all funny stories
and fell asleep on the couch. We were always sorry
when he left."

Grandpa Ball had a snowy white beard, and a long

skinny body. He knew how to find morels, and wild asparagus, ate young milkweeds in the spring, and green onions. He never had a bad word to say about the woman who left him, but there were others who did.

It was said of Edna she had "known" many other men besides the man she had run off with, including a cousin of the Irish poet, Thomas Moore, from Fiddletown; and that once in Montreal, where she went on a shopping trip to the Hudson Bay Company, she had been with two men at the same time, trappers from the North Shore of the St. Lawrence, and they had been "seen" together, drunk, in one of the private dining rooms of "an Establishment."

People also said she'd been with Eben's father and his brother.

Of course, they also accused Eben of being half-witted and addle-brained. They said he bragged a lot as a young man about his powers and was virtually impotent.

Then where had all of Edna's nine children been spawned?

They were Eben's, people insisted. That was about all he was good for: one shots.

I know some distant descendants of the Balls who, even to this day, like to tell tales about Edna. How she never had to pay to have any of her children examined by the doctor, because he was a boyfriend, and about how other of her lovers furnished the family with shoes, hats, winter mittens, galoshes, and curtains.

Over the front door of the Ball house in Gansevoort was a wooden placard with red letters burnt into it: SPARLING. Edna's mother's family were Sparlings from Chestertown. The Sparlings were said to be very shrewd in business, dangerous in love, and, otherwise, untrustworthy. No Sparlings were ever convicted of specific crimes or malfeasances, but Guy Sparling, it was said, once killed a man in Rimouski, Quebec, in a lumber deal and got away with it. They were a fierce thick clan of folk and Eben was definitely a stranger in their midst, even with his own wife. I picture him coming home for supper from his day at the Blacksmith's Shop and walking beneath that large placard to open his own front door. Edna is not about the house. The children don't know where she may have gone off to. It is certainly not her day at the Creamery. Eben warms some soup for himself and falls asleep in the easy chair by the fire. When Edna comes home she scolds him for his muddy feet, and says she's going up to bed. He can join her if he likes, but he had better behave himself. "I've had enough nonsense for one day," Edna says.

In March, which was mud-season, 1893, Eben Ball left home to go on a business trip to Schenectady. He was then in yard goods and buying cloth. Before leaving on the early morning trolley, he wrote a note for his wife:

"My beloved wife, I have to go away to buy some cloth. I trust you and the children will be well in my absence. I have infinite faith in your infinite capacities, and entrust you to the care of yourselves and the Good Lord. Farewell, as I shall only be a little while . . . Eben."

When he returned four and a half years later she was living with that other man near Elizabethtown; some people say Keene Valley. The children were grown and scattered. Eben was an old man, hardly remembered by the people in Gansevoort, and Bacon Hill.

Where had he been?

What had he been doing?

According to accounts in the Hargis and Gilpin family diaries, Eben had another woman and another family for a while in Southeastern Ohio in a place called Adena, and then had wandered further west to the gold fields of Canada, returning by ship, finally, around Cape Horn.

He had not struck it rich. He was very lean and bedraggled, and nobody ever says of Eben, then or now, that he went off with another woman.

What they did say is written on his gravestone for all to see:

> "This simple man
> got in over his head
> in death, as he did in bed.
> Now buried for all
> eternity,
> he'll soon return
> to his simplicity."

Ardis Elihu
* *
 *

An Italian immigrant woman called Ardis Elihu came to the County in 1881 from the regions to the south of Italy, and possibly Naples, and immediately set herself up in business in the Falls in a house of ill repute.

She was an immediate success among the better class of males and was protected and admired, and soon she had confederates and employees. Her large bay-windowed house on Upper Bay Street, across from the pharmacy, conveniently enough, was handsomely appointed in oaks and velvets; and there was a black maid to serve drinks, and a valet to see to the men's clothes.

Ardis Elihu practiced her cunning trade for more than twenty years in Glens Falls, and was so accepted after a while by the respectable folk of the town that she was finally able to make a union with Lawyer Salem (Slam) Porvarnicz, and they moved away to Saratoga.

But before she bowed herself in wedlock to Porvarnicz, she was any man's whore *for a price*, and a fabulous one, at that, to judge from comments of the day: tall and shapely, full-bosomed, with deep auburn reddish locks and a complexion the color of cocoa butter.

She was always lavishly dressed, handsomely groomed, and richly perfumed. She was the *première* exponent of *l'amour français* and *l'amour grec*, and by her proficiency in these arts made many a local housewife irritable, and jealous.

She tried hard not to disrupt marriages and would often attempt to pay a call on certain women whose husbands had spent the night with her; but, of course, she was not received until Porvarnicz, a Polish immigrant whose father served with Kosciusko, offered her his hand.

Ardis Elihu spoke with a very heavy Continental accent in a deep low tremolo. She had a carriage with a pair of white horses that she kept beplumed, and a her coachman in his livery boasted of the colors of the Italianate Savoy.

She was never raided, and never publicly humiliated, except for those times when she called on injured domestic parties, and it was rumored that she had a protector in one of the Pruyns of the paper and lumbering empire. This was never proved. She was also said to be very musical and could make her bosoms swing in opposite directions to Strauss waltzes, polkas, mazurkas. *Tutti Quanti.*

Whenever she walked out on the streets unaccompanied by a servant or one of her gentlemen, she was whistled at by the local schoolboys who cast balls of dung her way in the summer, and in the wintertime snow balls, and there were very often rocks.

In 1895 she journeyed to Italy and returned with her widowed mother and her brother, Silencio, a mute. These she set up in a separate establishment on Ridge Street.

In 1896 she presented to one and all a recently

arrived gentleman from abroad, Count Eliscu, whom she claimed was a direct descendant of Pope Innocent II.

He lived in her establishment and had certain exotic undefined duties which made him very popular among the better classes, indeed legendary.

In 1897 Ardis Elihu was sued for alienation of affections for more than twenty thousand dollars by the widow of Ten Eyck Brass. The suit was dropped for lack of specific proofs, but during the course of pretrial testimony it came out that the Elihus and the Eliscus were cousins from Rumania, in particular the city of Kishinev in Bessarabia, and their connections to crime and vice had been longstanding.

Shortly thereafter, Ardis met and married Porvarnicz, and Eliscu left for New York City. The house and the property on which it stood was sold to a confederate, Mrs. Eldrite, a portly Canadian woman, and is today a dentist's office, though no longer in the Eldrite family.

Little Rose Of Sharon
& Evelyn DeVilbliss
* *
*

Little Rose of Sharon & Evelyn DeVilbliss were lovers by common knowledge: that is to say, they lived together openly in Fort Edward for nearly thirty years and they probably made love fairly often.

"The girls," as they were commonly called, were in their late twenties when they met. Irish Rose was short and dainty and fair; Evelyn was dark and heavy-set and sweetfaced, with large glowing mysterious dark eyes and a faint downy brown mustachio. They kept an Airedale bitch, grew the best pole beans in town during the summer, and their various cucumber and watermelon relishes were acclaimed by all.

You could almost see the passion leap between them at times "like sparks," according to one contemporary. They were, in his words, "the oddest pair of swains our town had ever seen." But they were never persecuted and rarely fulminated against. On occasion they even went to the Congregationalist Church together on Sunday, and since both worked at an insurance company in Glens Falls as stenographers they always took the trolley to work together, sitting cozily side by side along the bumpy ride like a pair of "clubby ten pins, or Indian clubs." Nobody ever speculated about their life together, or what they did together, for the record, except to say, as Rev. Dr. Weymouth did once, at a ladies' tea, that there "were many worse citizens in Fort Edward than that sweet old pair."

They were friends, as well as lovers. Nobody ever knew of any discords between them; they were thick as treacle, and good to everybody who approached them except Brubaker, the knife and scissors grinder. He was not permitted to come to their house, much less knock on their door, and he always claimed to the day of his death to know secrets about them which the townspeople, of course, were only too eager to ignore.

There weren't really that many openly unusual arrangements in Fort Edward, and very little open male homosexuality, although there were always the rumors about Rev. Dr. Weymouth and the high-school boys, and about Slobbery Bob, the druggist's son, later killed in Mexico with Pershing's army. There were no open transvestites, no fags, no Nancies, sissies, or queers, but once in a while the local boys went down to the feeder canal in high summer of an evening and smoked jimson weed and had what was always called "a gay old time together just with themselves." Probably that involved many a cock-pull and who knows what else. . . .

From the now-defunct Hudson Falls gazette for July 10, 1900, I read of a "wiener party on the lawn of Herman Moll of Pearl Street ending in fisticuffs." The same paper reports that Rose of Sharon & Evelyn DeVilbliss had been awarded gold-filled spectacle cases for "twenty years of faithful service to Glens Falls Insurance Co." at a tea at the home of Mrs. Frederick Uppman Bass of Queensbury, attended by their sister employees and officers and fellow employees of the Company.

What else do we know of Little Rose & Evelyn? They left their fortunes to each other, with no other heirs mentioned, and died only weeks apart, thereby enriching the relatives they did not know in Binghamton, New York, and Elmira, and Cropseyville, as well as the Comptroller of New York State.

Also, they were known to have given away significant sums in charity to the homeless men of the vicinity during their lifetimes.

They always fed their Airedale "the best quality steak, as well as beef hearts," and their large joint tombstone, in the shape of a marble Psyche, naked, reads, at its base, significantly, "Friends."

"Sheeny Mike" Abbot
* *
*

It doesn't sound like a Jewish name, but he was, according to all the locals: "full-blooded," as they are also prone to speak of Indians in Washington County. "Sheeny Mike" Abbot had a big hook of a nose, a big Jewboy thing, too, that "frightened many a woman," and he went from door to door in the County selling laces, bindings, and "trims."

His calling card is preserved in one local historical society: "Sheeny Mike has something for every householder at a price she can afford. Custom orders taken."

He lived to be one hundred and seven, according to the local legend, and died in the poorhouse in Argyle from "pulmonary complications."

His long-time mistress was called Big Albany, but her name was Sylvia. She was also rumored to be Israelite, and she died in the Greenwich Old Ladies' Home during a smoky fire after living many years in Greenwich, Salem, and Shushan.

They had one issue: the "I Cash Clothes Man" Morey.

Charley Long Sleeves

Had two brothers; Charley Short Sleeves, and Charley One Arm. Both became Albanians, but Charley Long Sleeves stayed on in Bacon Hill to run the family farm. He made a little money and married a Battenburg woman name of Jane Wonderling. For a while they prospered in pigs. Jane was famous locally for her May baskets, and Chocolate Cocoanut Divinity cakes.

The family farm has been passed on down through five more generations. Present occupants sell night crawlers.

"Boiley Yam"

* *
*

A highwayman flourished in the 1880s in the area between Moreau and Wilton. He was called "Boiley Yam" because of an odd reddish-orangy complexion. The name, in which the past tense has been dropped, is also a corruption of the Irish proper name Bailey.

Notorious for his arrogance and enterprise, "Boiley Yam" would most often strike unsuspecting wayfarers as they were stopping to relieve themselves in a copse beside the road. Upon finding them so occupied, and disarmed, he would accost them with drawn poignard, bowie knife, or a revolver.

"He took only property," it is said, "and showed his respect for life by always waiting until the wayfarer had completed all of his (or her) hygienic necessities before relieving them of cash, and other such property."

> "Boiley yam Boiley yam
> Come and get me here I am!"

a nonsense rhyme of the period, to which children often played hide-and-seek, is preserved in those words. He was said to be well over six feet in height, and wore rings on all his fingers belonging to his various victims; and his hideout in the woods near Stillwater was known only to the villain, and his most trusted confederates, whose names have not survived him.

"Boiley Yam" volunteered to serve with Colonel Roosevelt's Rough Riders in the expeditionary force to the Caribbean and was never heard from again in Washington, Warren, or Saratoga Counties.

Legend has it that he remained behind after the war was over in Cuba and invested a large sum of cash in holdings of sugar and tobacco.

The Boleg Twins
* *
 *

Hungarians, they introduced hot red peppers to the
County. They were noted for their "canker sores" and
bad teeth, and were called Tom and Attlee, although
christened Tomasz and Attila. Tom was three inches
shorter than Attlee, but they were otherwise identical except that Attlee suffered from rickets.

   They are buried together in Renssalaer County in
the parish yard at Buskirk in a family plot contributed
by relatives.

Elder Black & Elder Noble
* *
 *

Noble was black, and Black was not ignoble: this pair
of Mormon brothers from somewhere in the region
between Upper Saranac Lake and Little Tupper consisted of a runaway octoroon slave from the Carolinas
and his comrade, master, and protector. Having survived bondage, manumission, and the hazardous underground railway, Noble came to pass as a fellow
Mormon of more than usual pigmentation, and Black
declared him to be his cousin and friend. Still, they
were renowned more for the oddities of their names
and complexions than for any particular anecdotes I
can here dispense.

Neither man ever married.

After a while in Plattsburgh, where they owned a
profitable tannery, they sold out to the Jews and
bought up considerable acreage in the area around
Middle Falls where they raised melons, shipping them
south in season along the canal to Albany and New
York.

Both men grew quite wealthy, as we know from a
contemporary account: In the year 1882—according
to the Schuylerville paper—the London goldsmith
Pastini was commissioned by the two Elders to have
printed on gold-leaf pages a hand-blocked version of
the Mormonite Book of Mormon.

Their house is now a Phillips 66 station, and the once extensive farm acreage, extending all the way to the village of Malta, has been subdivided.

They were nicknamed "Elder Kith and Kin," and are buried just across the canal from Fort Edward on sanctified ground a few hundred yards from a Hess Oil Company station.

Everett Mole

* *
*

"He had an eye in his ass," they said of Everett Mole, meaning, I suppose, he was rather of a suspicious nature (and with reason) and could see backwards, as if to ward off the evil spirits.

But was he not always dressed? Did he not wear clothes? Pants? Trousers? Or knickers?

Whenever I have asked, the metaphor seems to disintegrate. Everett, it seems, was a very tattered man, a man of rags, but he did hide nearly all of his nakedness in something. Then people will say, "Probably he flinched a lot, you know. We still use the expression."

I picture him then as large, stoop-shouldered, sluglike, almost, like microscopic photos of the E-colis bacteria, only a mass of shivers and flinches. He was bug-ridden, and nervous, a twitcher, nibbling and cribbling, desperate, and despised. Sort of the laughingstock of the area around 1910:

> "An eye in his ass
> and he winked and
> passed gas."

By trade a common laborer, Everett had no wife, and no acknowledged children. He was born in French Canada, and died, apparently, a suicide, of an overdose of laudanum administered to relieve the pain of a limb severed when he fell between the wheels of a D & H locomotive on the bridge outside Fort Ann.

Everett Mole lived forty-eight years in and around Washington and Warren Counties as common laborer, bung-tapper, hog-boiler, and butcher's helper, and legend has it he never owned an overcoat. He wore sweaters, rags, and more sweaters, spoke with a lisping French accent. His nicknames were "strawberry" and "lummox." He was called "Dopey Benny" and "Hooknose," though he was not a Jew. There were really very few Jews in the Counties at the time and they were chiefly storekeepers. Everett had no living relatives and few friends. Nobody ever mentions him in diaries and letters except for Noella Boggs who simply writes to a friend in Schenectady in one of her chatty weekly communications, "The Old Black Mole took his life after a horrible accident. God rest his ugly soul at last, he'll not be bothering any of us local housewives any more."

Mole's tombstone reads: *E. Mole, laborer, 48 years of earth to suffer.*

How he was buried, who paid for the funeral, and the small white tombstone, we don't know; nor can we be sure that Noella spoke of Everett in her letter to her friend; bad accidents were an almost everyday occurrence among the laboring classes, and suicides were the most persistent cure for winter loneliness.

My own mother used to say, "The winter takes some peoples' lives away."

She also used to say, "dumb like the Mole," meaning the laborer, not the rodent.

When I asked her once where she had picked up such an expression, she said she had always used it. She had lots of expressions like that: "salty smoke" referred to a popular way of treating the local pork, and "fat as a carbuncle" meant, to her way of thinking, a trolley barn. Also, "in the vaseline jar" meant stuck, and a "good five-pounder" referred to any excessive expulsion of gas in the presence of polite company, a common wintertime amusement before the invention of the Ski-Do.

As Mother always said, "The fairer sex are never very fair." If Everett Mole even really bothered any of the local women he was never arrested, or fined. Probably his uncouth stature and drudging daily occupations suggested such fears in other peoples' minds. Also, for a short while, we know he delivered meats for the Atlantic & Pacific market on Upper Glen Street, and then he may have been called Bloody Mole, as many butchers' men were, because in those days beef was always freshly slaughtered and freshly quartered and the joints ran with blood in the hands of the helpers. Gristled and grizzly, and begored, Everett had to enter many a respectable Falls household, and may have been a fearful sight. For a short while, he lived in lodgings on John Street in Sandy Hill until complaints were lodged against him for "harboring maggots."

Like Dick Diver, he finally passed into history somewhere near the Falls, a figure of legend and loathing, odd, foul, pestilential, uncouth, with eyes in his ass and a hearty five-pounder to greet his fellows. There's a song I've heard schoolchildren still singing in Moreau when they jump rope or play tag near the old Union Bag factory:

> "Better watch out
> Old Mole gonna get you
> with his great big

bloody finger he'll get you.
Get you with a five-
pounder till you pass out.
Watch for old Mole
in the tar patches,
and in the scratches
in the brickworks, and
in the woods between
the birches. Old Mole
he'll get you if
you don't watch out!"

Felicity Hapgood
* *
 *

She kept sheep, for the Watsons, as many years as her limbs would carry her, and when she couldn't any longer, married; and, shortly thereafter, she was dead.

That is all we really know of Felicity Hapgood, a shepherdess among the Argyle hills, until she moved to Fort Edward to marry Everett Plumly when she came down with a pox that had been in the family and passed on with him, or shortly thereafter, to her eternal rest.

Felicity's tombstone records:

"Felicity Hapgood
died of the fever.
Her sheep rove on
beside the river."

Everett's tombstone is simpler, stark by comparison, a matter of dates: "1844–1896."

They left no heirs.

But of those fifty-two years of Everett's life we know a great deal, about his vast real-estate holdings in Albany and Round Lake (from titles and deeds), and of his management of a brewery in his early twenties in Lake Skaneateles in Western New York.

By one contemporary, Everett Plumly was remembered as "brawny but fine, enterprising, a Citizen of the Republic of widespread interests."

In the diaries of Freelove Herrison we learn he prospected for coal throughout the region along with certain members of the Gansevoort clan, always unsuccessfully, and that eventually some surviving members of his pox-decimated family established themselves in that line of work in Southeastern Ohio.

There is also this curious entry: "Met Ev for a walk. All very customary and usual. Nonsense about holding hands, true friends for life, love eternal, and thence to Gansevoort where we were forever briefly in the churchyard."

With no certainty can we surmise what Freelove might have surmised as "forever," or what acts pertained to the beyond—beyond what was momentary, improvisatory, possibly premonitory.

We have a note of salutation, lacking a farewell, and a note of farewell, lacking any salutation: "There is no contrived state of war between us. I don't want to see you. No battles, no truces, no explanations needed. Don't write or call on me again."

Poor Felicity was still a shepherdess at that time and Everett was young, and strong, a hearty man, just coming into his patrimony. They were not among the "young gay crowd" of Washington County pleasure-seekers who picnicked on the shores of Lake Cossayuna and took their pleasures, in the words of one rather envious chronicler, "amidst the sylvan delights, catch as catch can."

In the Herrison diaries one reads: "Took myself to do a certain thing with E. on his shay and I was left at the cross-roads, rather pleased with myself, though damp."

From numerous letters preserved in the library of the State Historical Society one learns of "divine F," "astonishing F," "willful Felice," and the "insouciant Shepherdess." But just as we cannot ascertain who the E. in Freelove's life was with any proof, we must remain aware of the possibility of more than one shepherdess among the Argyle hills with F. as her principal initial.

Scholars are not more free to judge the moral behavior of their subjects from the allusive chicken scratchings in their diaries than are we to believe in the truth of lies that are passed down among us in our families because they pretend to be History.

What we know of Felicity we know chiefly from blanks, empty spaces surrounding the fact that she was born, worked, married, and died. She was mother of nobody and really wife to nobody. In those days it might have been assumed that she hardly existed.

1860–1896: an arduous passage through mystery about time that yields us no answers except through death.

Caleb Ganthem

*
* *

This follower of John Brown from Salem was not so dedicated or ferocious as his master: he'd been a slaver once himself.

We know he traced some of his lineage to the British poet, Fulke Greville.

He wrote a pamphlet entitled "On The Beastification of Some Men" and published it privately. As was the custom in those days.

He argued, from a copy in my possession, that "we are all much more simply human than otherwise," a naive but charming conviction; and that the true, and perhaps only, liberation of his fellow whites from their racist preoccupations must come about through a [homosexual?] contact between white and black male adolescents which he referred to as "ineffable experience of an educative nature."

He eventually moved himself further North and West to the "burned over" district of the State, where religious controversies raged well into the end of the last century, and we hear nothing more of him except, by way of a disciple, who encountered him casually while passing through the area, that "he was extremely hospitable, but would (himself) eat no fowl larger than a chicken."

Olive Ryder

* *
 *

By a freak of nature Olive Ryder was born without the female part, and had to be content to be a spinster throughout her rather short life. Nevertheless, she carded and dyed wool, and sold firewood, to provide for her limited needs; and she kept herself clean, and warm, and well-nourished until the frost of 1884 when she perished in her small house two miles from Fort Edward.

She was said to be a very pretty lady, and many men who did not know of her affliction during her life wooed her and were sorely disappointed.

Olive Ryder had a sister Jo in Sandy Hill who sometimes came to visit her after the death of their parents, and she was very well-liked by ministers of all faiths and the laity, under the circumstances, but they finally all managed to neglect her, including Jo, and she perished.

She was never heard to utter a single bright saying, or an unkind word, and was thought by all virtuous, and on her small white marble headstone is carved: "Here lies one who was without fault in her life and in death shall have no peers."

Vanessa Wunderlich
* *
*

She was pretty, but said to be vague. Men admired her good looks, and wondered if she ever took any notice of their attentions. She lived with her family, and they took fine care of her, clothed her and fed her well and welcomed any and all suitors, until her teeth started to rot in her mouth, and that face, like a cameo, started to sink into itself in reverse, hardly seeming to be in relief at all any more.

The poor thing was suffering from an infection that venereally gnawed at her gums. It came from what she had once eaten, in a rash moment, at her cousin Ellen's house in Chestertown: the hair pie, or so was I told. . . .

No wonder she was so vague. Cousin Ellen married, and died in child bed: poxy. Nessa didn't like to remember such a lovely peculiar taste to which she was constrained by custom and tradition from seeking more of the same, or other alternates.

I was neighbored to her twenty years or more and once she broke out from her vaguery to call me "an old fag" in irritation at my dog, Brewster; and I never forgave her for that, but when she died, before her time, and with her spinster knot in tight tangles, I wept at her funeral and wished her well in the life to come, if there be one, as a mouse, or a snail, or a poached egg.

She taught in the Grammar School, eighth grade, and many of the local boys took on crushes because her figure remained handsome long after that face wizened on her; of the local little girls who were her pupils and what they did with her I do not know because it is not so strange in the County for young women to nip at each other like dogs and pussy cats, and nobody will usually say "for shame," unless it be in the head of that person herself; because such a woman is, too often, thought of as "the man without," and what on earth is the good of that except, maybe, "for pleasuring . . . if there be any," as my old friend Crow Marie used to say. . . .

Lace Curtains
* *
*

Lacey (Lace) Curtains began as a drayman and became a joiner. In short order he was a cooper, a puddler, a mason, a hod carrier, a pedlar, a pinch bottler, and a short-order cook. Lace flailed wheat and farmed fennel. He was a boilerman, a pot stiller, and a punchboard collector, repaired Wurlitzers and Atwater Kent wireless radios, and wove and patched caneback chairs. He had an abiding interest in the Mexican gold half-peso, which he collected, when he could, and old wax Zimmerman consolette recording cylinders, conducted Bingo games, leaf tours in the fall, and grew chrysanthemums for the high-school football "boosterettes." In the winter he harvested Christmas trees, was the check-out at the Grand Union, and pumped gas for Cumberland Farms.

This simple yeoman, a perfect amalgam of industry and thrift, lacked only one thing: skillfulness, and craft. He was, in fact, a bit of a bungler, and gollywoggler. A bad drunk, too. In his last years he raised pregnant mares for their urine which was then used in the synthesis of birth control pills.

Lace had none of the advantages of the educated man and it showed. Whatever he put his hands to he usually failed at: his barrels leaked and his walls would not stay up. When he plucked ducks and dipped sheep the poor creatures usually died before their appointed times. But in his later years he collected many a brimming stoop of urine and prospered, until a mare kicked him almost fifty feet and he had to retire.

Well, you know, he died miserable and poor, and he even lacked good will. People said they stopped caring for Lace when he overcharged them at the Grand Union.

Lace always said the most important thing he owned was his last name. If drunk, he would sometimes add: "It will be curtains for you, too, my man, if you don't learn to respect that."

He was also quoted as saying: "When I die I want to be that TV fellow, George Plimpton. Queen For A Day."

Needless to say, he had a son with Rose Edmundson and they called the lad Bledsoe, and when I asked why, Lace explained: "Because it's Eosdelb backwards."

Fred McBaine

****** ****
 *

Lately, whenever I hear the word Culture, I reach for
the name Fred McBaine. He was cultural all the way
from here to Albany, went to Italy every summer
with his loony wife, and spoiled rotten son, to study
the goddam Renaissance, and believed in all the right
things: Literature, the Arts.

I always thought Fred was a cold fish, a typical
outlander from the Berkshires with maple syrup running through his veins, or maybe snow. He came up to
Hudson Falls to become the Dean of the Community
College and everybody wondered how come such a
high-toned guy, with degrees from Princeton, and
Cambridge, England, would want to live in our
County. Then it turned out he had a number of bad
habits: like that wife, whom he had removed from the
care of the psychiatrist and kept doped up inside a
sweat box he'd built. Mac had an abiding interest in
right-wing politics. Now when I say right wing for the
County I mean right wing: Fred was no ordinary GOP
supporter, or loud mouth Buckley-ite. He was an outright fascist, but polite about it as a never-you-mind,
thought General Franco was a great man, and so—he
believed—Marshal Stalin.

Mac admired power. So he chose to be this whale in
a minnow pond. He flunked any student who didn't

kowtow toward him, and then he started writing a book. Called it *Toward an Arab Solution, Finally, in the Middle East*, based on his various trips abroad to Beirut, Lebanon, and Dubai, where he had a sister, but some local merchants got wind of what he was about from an interview in the papers and they decided what he meant was *The* Final Solution. That didn't make him any friends on Main Street, and he was finally asked to look for other work.

Well, he got himself a job at a college further upstate in Saranac called Roger Smith and for all I know he is still there: teaching Humanities to the pulp & paper students. He may even publish that book someday and make himself a big name in New York and end up a Dean of Foresters. He looked very distinguished: always wore a watchfob in the vest of his tailored suits, and served you French wines and cheese at his receptions.

He had some funny ideas: like Herbert Lehman and Al Smith started World War II; and his favorite writings were a German mystic and doctor name of Hans Carossa, and the Tibetan Book of Prayer, and the classical physician Galen.

When he lived up here a lot of people used to come and visit him from abroad, such as college professors, and other learned men. People said he fooled around with young women.

Wilhelm Vershlag,
Tract Writer
* *
 *

When that hour draws nigh which shall close the business of life, and summon the spirit to the bar of "God who gave it," all the motives to deception cease; and those false reasonings which blind the judgment are dissipated. Such moments are the elements of profit.

It is the hour of truth and sincerity.

Such, at least, was the general fact for Wilhelm Vershlag, a German immigrant writer of tracts who came to Sandy Hill in 1861 and published copiously more than one hundred ninety essays against sin and enlightened ideas that were circulated throughout the Capitol area, and the three Counties.

Vershlag was much intoxicated with death, his own, and others. His concerns were not invalidated by an ever-pressing knowledge that some men have been found to cherish their infatuation with wickedness and practice their knavery until the very last.

He wrote tracts against the ideas of Hume and Finley, against Saint-Simonianism, and the practice of divorce. He inveighed against carnal love, infidelism (or the study of Eastern Religions and Mysticism), and female suffrage. He reproached the anti-slavers as going beyond the provenance of their Maker, and declared of the Swedenborgians that they were making premature that "state of untried being which lies before us all."

His most memorable line was, I think, "death becomes an object of unutterable moment."

He was virtuous and clean himself, and a prodigious toiler. He spared no effort to write and distribute his tracts, and preach from them to one and all, including on their back covers, for example, reproachful replies to the "infidel" Lord Byron and others, so as to seduce his audiences to read what lay between his covers.

Vershlag was poor, but never down-and-out. He farmed, and could provide for himself and his family; and he repaired shoes and made rainboots from greased cowhides which he sold for 75¢ the pair. Eventually he also had subscribers and even sponsors and benefactors among the dairying families, and among the local bourgeoisie.

He was married twice and both wives died young.

He had five children, and a red dog named Tom who went with him everywhere to whom he was said to be much devoted.

In fact, unschooled, he was self-educated, and an autodidact of the European sort who could even read a Hebrew bible, and some Aramaic.

He died in a snowstorm outside Troy of an embolism after being snow-blinded, and his children were all sent to the County orphanage.

His tombstone reads: "Turn away from the philosopher to hear what a believer in the Lord Jesus Christ has to say."

Surrogate Fury

* *
*

Walter Jackett Fury, Justice, was Judge of the New York State Supreme Court, Washington County Surrogate, a member of the Ennis-Brown clan from Ogdensburg, and one of the leading practitioners of the New York State Bar.

Between 1860 and 1892 he was never out of public office.

He was a small stubby man who lost one ear in a hunting accident while still in college at Dartmouth, and he wore his sandy hair long and thick.

Justice Fury collected knives.

He married six times and none of his wives were with him for longer than a month.

It is said that "while otherwise gentle, mild, scholarly, and self-effacing, a true worthy of the great traditions of the State Bar, his marital practices were considered loathsome and repugnant to most wholesome women."

The specific details of how he comported himself in his domestic affairs were never revealed by any of the fine women of good family and bearing with whom he would unite himself, howsoever briefly, and the two wives who survive him to this day in Whitehall and Smith's Basin have refused comment of any sort.

A portrait of Justice Fury survives and it shows a

slightly pockmarked face, and a little half-smile that may have been subterfuge for untold malevolences, as the artist was a local woman, Emilia Bangs Shaw.

Surrogate Fury traveled widely throughout the States and on the Continent. He was licensed to read at Gray's Inn, London, and the University of Bologna, Italy. He was a 32-degree Mason.

A Presbyterian by conviction, as well as ardent faith, he wrote an important early monograph that was much admired on the introduction of European strains among the dairymen of Washington County, and stood for his party's nomination for Governor twice, unsuccessfully.

It was said that his oddly irregular personal life did not do him yeoman service in the political arena, and after 1886 he never again was prominent as a figure in statewide politics.

Jackett Fury's collection of model trains was one of the largest in the Eastern United States.

His last years were spent in the company of his housekeeper, Madge Hoggit.

He left a considerable fortune in real property and convertible debentures.

His only son, Graham, is branch manager of a bank in Schenectady.

His favorite saying was, "The Mormonite Duck is monogamous."

Gogi Gandolfo
* *
*

Gogi Gandolfo was an Italian stonecutter who worked on the canals—like Barney Caine, I imagine—during the last century.

Nothing much is known about such people. They were superb artisans, engineers, and craftsmen, and did not signature their work except through legends.

In the churchyard of St. Marg's is a stone:

> "Gogi Gandolfo
>   Born in Tuscany, 1832.
>   Died in Hudson Falls, 1900."

Must be the same fellow.

There are no other stones bearing that surname.

Must have been a bachelor button.

I've checked all the local directories and there doesn't seem to be any Gandolfos about locally any more, so if he had any heirs they must have all died or moved away.

John Stout
* *
*

He was walleyed, and had a hang tooth, yet the women liked him. They claimed to find him fascinating. They said he had a really big one, and could go forever with only a pause for meals, or the calls of nature.

He never married except once to a sister of the Reckins clan from Gloversville where he lived a year or more but she grew tired of all his infidelities and then the brothers demanded he leave her forever.

It was his custom, people said, to take as many as three or four different women a day well into his fifties. The townspeople said it was just his way, is all, and seemed to understand. Besides, by then, he may have had most of their wives and sisters.

John Stout maintained he could get along with men as friends, if he had to, but could only be with a woman if he and she were making love, and he wished above all to be "friendly."

He made a good living as a chemist in my father's paper mill and always dressed in the style of the dandy: waxed calf shoes from Peal Company, New York; a bowler hat; and spats. He carried a cane, too, with an onyx knob topped by a large crystal ball from Bavaria, but many women have told me it was that eye of his that was the selling point. They never knew if it was looking at them or not, and they found themselves, pretty soon, trying to attract its attention, and that's when he would put it to them.

A strange man this: I never knew him to have any other recreation.

He lived in a flat in the Queensbury Hotel on the top floor and ate Sunday dinners at their Smorgasbord Buffet, and he was always known to take a Manhattan before his meal except on New Year's Eve when he would have a Rye Old Fashioned without sugar.

"Priceless" Abbot
* *
*

The brother of Bernadine, who was my classmate at Molly Stark: he was also a friend in need to most of the Howlands during the Great Crash.

I think they called him "Priceless" because the name was Price, but as he was pretty much of a halfwit they didn't just want to grant him all of that name unsullied.

The only other things I know about him are he worked for a while as a customer's man in the local brokerage, and then he taught Greek and Latin at the Hoosick School.

His sister moved to Buffalo after marrying, but he never did. Kept pretty much to himself, too. I think he had some sort of liaison with one of the mill girls, but maybe not. He was thin and wraithlike, and wore black suits, and detachable collars, really just dickies, I think, well into the Franklin Roosevelt years.

He took a subscription to the *North American Review*, the only one in our town, I believe, and claimed to be hard at work on a great opus which did not survive him.

We would meet at the Post Office where he rented a pigeon hole.

He was gap-toothed and his favorite expression was: "Beautiful day outside. Hope it stays that way until tomorrow so I can enjoy it."

Luddy Blake

* *
  *

I must remember to tell about little Luddy Blake by
quoting the poem we all wrote about her for Class Day
at Fort Edward High:

> "Luddy Blake
> Luddy Blake
> Were you just
> A Big Mistake?
> Were you born
> for penance sake?
> Drown in a lake
> Luddy Blake."

After graduation, this same Luddy removed herself from Fort Edward, and I heard years later that
she went on to acquire her *soupçon* of education at
Cornell, which was free for girls, and took a job with
the Telephone Company and became a supervisor,
marrying somebody from the Company, too. They
had one son, a doctor, and another who, I'm told, is a
hairdresser in Philadelphia.

I believe she's still alive and lives in some place like
Sun City, Arizona, and if anybody does know her by
reputation out there it's just as well they don't remind
her of that poem, as she may be leading a happy life.

Luddy called me Buck in high school, I don't know why.

She was always appointed bathroom monitor and she would report all the other kids.

Nota Bene: Luddy Blake looked a lot like my old classmate, Arnold Benjamin, which should not be too surprising when you realize both their mommas had Doctor Morgan for their lying-ins.

Whereas Arnold was a girlish blonde angelic version of the doctor (wide-eyed, angel-eyed, you might say), Luddy looked mean as hell, even as a kid, a jaw like a coon trap, Little Iodine eyes. I guess nowadays they would say the way she looked was boyish, or, maybe, hoydenish.

Mean as sin, we all used to say.

My own ma used to tell me such looks had a lot to do with whether a woman had a good or bad time conceiving of them.

She always swore Arnold looked like "the best damned cum" a woman could ever have.

Others she told me who had reason to look like old Doc Morgan were Paris Wasser, Vanessa W, Cack the Sissy, and Cameron Green (not mentioned otherwise in this narrative since he long ago left the County and is doing so well in the State House in Albany) and I guess none of these offspring really looked identical, though there were resemblances. I don't know. The doctor died after I was born, and Ma always said "only Arnold looked as if he had ever kissed a star."

A true history of Doctor Morgan is beyond my scope here. All I know for certain is he made a lot of money and most of the local women, when they had mounted his stirrups, chose his "raw beef injections," too, though Ma always said he had a gentle soul, the "warmest softest touch of any doctor ever," and was never "just forward" in his examining room but "understanding" and "kind": a true gentleman of the old school.

Morgan's daughter, Mary Claire, was left so well off she moved to one of those big houses on Grand Avenue in Saratoga, and ran her own "stud"—only, as the neighbors say down at Hattie's Chicken Shack over a plate of delicious fried oysters, "there are never any horses on or near the premises, even during racing season."

Morgan's Kids
* *
 *

These are some of the children of old Doc Morgan:

> Cack the Sissy
> Luddy Blake
> Griff Griffin
> Arnold Benjamin
> Paris Wasser
> Nessa W
> Cameron Green
> Gaylord Spinker (our distant cousin)
> Eulalie Economo
> Morgan Morgenbesser

To the best of my knowledge there are no others.

Morgan Morgenbesser took his degree in Civil Engineering at Columbia University in the Thirties, and worked on the Atomic Bomb, in some capacity, and then we heard he was a Red, and lost his perch, and moved to California where they are more tolerant about such things, and Vegetarianism, too.

The sister, Marian, married a monster of a man, Mazerowski, and they raise malamutes and huskies in either Ballston Spa, or Malta. I forget which.

Coleman Breezy

*
* *

A land surveyor, engineer, and organizer of sporting events, Coleman Breezy was one of the great dandies of ante-bellum Washington County. His popularity with women, his legendary exploits of strength and derring-do, and his unfailing shows of good humor, were the stuff of ordinary quotidian gossip. He was called "Snappy."

Born in Fort Miller, of a good but by no means wealthy family of glovers and hatters, Breezy attended the Fort Edward Academy as a boarding student, and, later, spent two years at Union College in Schenectady as a student of theology and law before choosing his profession as surveyor and engineer for which his only experience came from a brief position with the Boston & Maine railroad.

He trooped to the colors during the War Between the States, was wounded twice, at Bull Run and Shiloh, and returned home to the County a hero.

For a short while he thought of a career in politics, but an affair with a dancer at the Albany Light Opera considerably dampened his chances in those pious times, and the handsome Breezy turned to making money. He was a prodigious earner and a prodigious spender: His breakfast oysters were imported weekly by stagecoach from Chesapeake Bay, and his wines from Paris. He made frequent trips to the Continent, and once went around the world. His romances were legendary, too, and there was not a woman in the County, it was said, who would not gladly "have given herself to him, whether betrothed, married, or no."

In 1884 Coleman Breezy journeyed to Scandinavia and returned married. His bride was Swedish, a great beauty, and a woman of considerable wealth and carriage. Inge Breezy, as she was called, was loved and admired by all, and the Breezys became the most sociable couple throughout the area. Their parties were legends and their balls the stuff of romance and the Arabian Nights. For one such event, during racing season, Coleman had arranged that the entire New York Philharmonic play waltz music while the guests were served caviar from Persia, Long Island oysters, game from the North Woods, and, for dessert, mango-champagne ice cream.

Inge and Coleman Breezy were together less than two years when she died in childbirth of the Semmelweis fever. Shortly thereafter, Coleman shot himself in the mouth with his wide-bore elephant gun so that pieces of the back of his head were, in one account, "spattered against the red brocade walls of his elegant salon."

It came as an equally great shock to all of Washington County to discover that Breezy had died bankrupt, owing debts of more than $100,000.

Father Emmett Calcoon
* *
*

Although born to County Cork, Ireland, where his ancestors had once owned much good grazing land, and a title, the Reverend Father Emmett Calcoon came to Washington County at age thirteen an orphan, to be with distant kinsmen. He was fed and clothed, and taken in and sent to school, and then to board in the Albany Diocese, where he received a seminary education, before returning to serve his parishioners of St. Marg & St. Joseph's Church for thirty-five years.

Father Calcoon was a handsome autocratic man, very popular with females for his light tenor voice, and his very smooth pink complexion which reddened into a full blush whenever he said mass and took the sacrament.

It was said by one and all that Father Calcoon's voice was as "smooth as the silk in the Pope's purse." People said he shaved so close that there was left nothing rough about him, outwardly, save his defiance of evil. He had a baby's skin, the skin of a young fresh girl, that fair he was, and when he officiated at funerals or christenings or, as I say, mass, he always looked hot and fresh and spicy, as if from his bath, glowing all roseate and hazy, haloed.

My own mother (who was Congregationalist) had

her crush on him, I think, and once I believed him to be my real father, though never proven. Hardly likely! Father Calcoon enjoyed the company of women. He was a loyal Parnellite, and once he entertained Parnell with other chuchmen in Albany. He was tall and lean, with wide shoulders, and before his hair turned silvery grey he wore it slicked back under pomades.

For those days, there is no denying Father Calcoon was a liberal churchman, easy with all manner of dispensations and indulgences, except that he would permit no women to enter his church without long sleeves and a hat, and this man of considerable personal charm always got on well with all the other local clergy, including the Syrian Catholic, Father Casimir.

His parish house was the setting for numerous interfaith gatherings, and teas. He liked chamber music, and could play country airs on a spinet. His housekeeper was Lorna Brown, renowned for the quality of her baking, and there were no ugly rumors about this son of God because it was more or less accepted by everybody that just as such a handsome and vital servant of the Lord should have all his dietary needs satisfied by the likes of Lorna Brown with good English roast beef, mutton chops, Yorkshire puddings, plum and sour apple or green tomato pies, so there must be numerous other local creatures available to sate his most pleasant emotional needs.

We are told, "this was no pantywaist puerile capon, but a priapean saint, bold for his time, though no less of a gentlemen."

In 1884 Father Emmett Calcoon was made Monsignor Calcoon, and went to Rome and Ravenna.

He purchased, on behalf of the parish, one of the

first automobiles in Sandy Hill in 1905, a Duryea, and learned to drive it around by himself.

By 1905, also, a large number of French Canadians were joining his congregation and Father Calcoon learned some French so that he might take confessions and chat during pastoral visits to his parishioners.

There remained some friction between the Irish, Italian, and Central European Catholic members of Calcoon's church, and the new French-Canadian flotsam (who were so much the poorer and ill-educated); and there is no denying that Monsignor Calcoon, though he would take no sides, felt more at home among his own kind, but he always endeavored to be fair, loving, merciful, and to educate his masses in the ways of tolerance, even inviting priests from French Canada to preach to his parish and oversee the mass.

He was also on good personal terms with the area's only rabbi, Seymour Seigel Sassoon, and with the millionaire gambler Rothstein, who had a house in nearby Schroon. So close were his ties to the Jewish "sage of the Sagamore," as he was called in our local press, that after one particularly rainy spring, which had made ploughing difficult, some farmers devised of their friendship a ditty that was both exhortation and prayer:

Sassoon
& Calcoon
Calcoon &
Sassoon
pray
no more
monsoon
until the
new moon.

Emmett Calcoon, when I knew him, was in his late sixties, all silvery grey, like an eagle, but not a severe pietist, no wearer of the hair shirt. Charming and devout, he could be a leader without becoming an exhorter. He was known to take a sociable drink, and to offer spirits to his guests when they visited him in the parish house. The most popular Democrat in Washington County, it was even suggested at the time of Bryan's first election that he put himself up for Congress.

Said a local editorialist at the time of his passing, he was "a true man of God," though "first and foremost" a Man; "and if he sinned at all, it was as God's servant and with the expectation of God's mercy."

His favorite airs were, as I recall, "Kathleen Mavourneen," and "Donegal Fair." Once, during a Lenten sermon, he surprised the congregations of St. Marg & St. Joseph's by describing Purgatory: "It won't—in the words of that air—last a day and can't be forever," and then he proceeded to sing all of that air plus "The West's Awake" for his amused parishioners.

Another story I like about the father concerns a pretty local girl who came to see him after being seduced on a D & H sleeper by two men who told her they were Harvard Medical students named Brown and Smith.

The girl swore she had believed them both but woke to find them gone from the train in Albany Station, and she now felt they had deceived her with false names.

The father tried to be understanding but he asked would the girl wish to say what her own name was.

"Virginia," she said, "Virginia Jones. Why do you ask?"

"Because it sounds to me every bit as false as Brown and Smith, and so I doubt you ever were a virgin, or *one* man should have done ye!"

But he did not punish the young woman, making her to serve, for a while, in his household, as a helper to Lorna Brown, and cleaning woman.

Father Emmett Calcoon enlisted to serve with the 7th Regiment, New York State National Guard, in 1917 as chaplain, and was machine-gunned to death close to the front lines at Château-Thierry.

He is buried among the troops he must have served so well in a military cemetery in Belgium.

Rosa Armitage
* *
 *

A cross-grained face, short, and fat, with glassy eyes like peek stones and a bulbous nose; she became a force to be reckoned with in County affairs for a little while. No gentlewoman, and of no great means or education, she nevertheless had followers, mostly Peasoup women from Quebec like herself, because of her large and outspoken piety.

"If only the Almighty had her faith," they would say, even the Catholics like herself, of Rosa, who came south to work in one of the tissue mills around 1873 and married with another Frenchy worker, Jean Santager.

They produced five children, and she was an excellent housewife, too, and mender of clothes, and kitchen gardener, though she gave over all her Sundays and moments of respite to a contemplation of the Living God.

In 1897, with her children all but one having left home, Rosa Armitage had a vision.

She claimed to speak with God; that he required her to establish a Papist school for the dissemination of his teachings.

She being an illiterate, her announcement was regarded at first with some scorn when she stood at Sunday mass to share her Vision with the others.

Father Emmett Calcoon advised that her soul was in peril if she be not seated.

But God, Rosa declared, was not a bookworm, not even a book-learner; he had instructed his son to be a carpenter, a fisherman; and he was pitifully rent by wounds and festering sores that had not healed ever since the crucifixion of that only son . . .

Father Calcoon reiterated that her continuing folly placed her soul and his, and every member of the congregation's, in mortal peril.

Rosa said she spoke not for herself but for a Divinity "larger than Mount Marcy," and she wished to know if she could show one and all certain infamous stones found in her backyard which she called her "luminous prayer stones" that were helpful to her, she said, in prolonging "such Divine visitations, and their intensity, and spasmodicity."

Father Calcoon asked all to withdraw and then demanded Rosa go also; he had his very own plans for schools, and diocesan approval. But she was, in his own words, "irrepressible." She soon quit work at the mill, and went about town collecting funds for the school. The Holy Healer School, as she called it, would instruct "us all in beatitude and Grace, so that our children will go blessedly forth to new prospects."

Some fifteen thousand dollars was collected, no mean sum in those days, and she had many silly woman rally to her, when she fell ill, and suffered violent apoplexies and drooling, as if she was "rabid." Then she called the good Father Calcoon to her bedside and told him, as he had always suspected, that her great project and the visions from which it sprang were the "products of my illicit imaginings."

She explained that with her children grown she did

not wish to return to the drudgery of the mill. But she said "it did not take me long to believe in this myself, so that, after a while, there was no discrepancy between mere truth and my visions."

She was offered extreme unction in return for the monies she had raised, and the story of her great despite was never made public, but she was treated as a local saint, and some would swear her body did not putrify.

Rosa was quoted in the Episcopal Church Bulletin, and the Methodists said she was "a good Catholic." Around Palmyra, New York, they erected a grave monument to her and she was finally reburied there.

But at her funeral Father Emmett Calcoon declared that "she may have hung out her wash with all the Higher Powers."

A school was eventually built in the Falls, but not as Rosa had required.

Her gravestone is in French: *"Rosa Marie Armitage. Seulement le commencement à sa propre histoire, à son propre secret."*

"Shake" Kelly
* *
*

"Shake" Kelly never worked. He made what little money he needed gambling; the name refers to a shaking of the dice.

He was very elegant, always wore a camel's-hair topcoat, even in the summer, and patent-leather low shoes.

He had no regular place of habitation or employment, but boarded among his low-life friends, and ran what amounted to a floating crap game between the Falls, Hudson Falls, and Fort Edward, in the Oddfellows lodges, Masonic halls, and various other places of confraternity.

He was arrested only once, for loitering in the Town of Wilton, by State Police and received a suspended sentence.

He was a popular and colorful character for many years from the turn of the century until the Depression years, and had numerous odd locutions and expressions that became a part of the local vocabulary, such as, "What we'll sometime see," to describe the indefinite future, such as it was and might be, and "the receding hairline of Fate" to describe the gambler's odds.

He never married, but in 1932 met a woman named Chugalug in a local tavern and they went off together West.

One story I particularly like about "Shake" concerns his fairness. Playing against a pair of loaded dice with a couple of visiting firemen at the Sagamore on Bolton Landing, "Shake" was rapidly divested of his small grub stake. He knew he had been had. He was furious. But rather than spoil the occasion with acrimony (and possibly mar his further welcome at that then-fabulous spa where he often made small fortunes on a single summer weekend), Kelly as he took his leave removed his pants and handed them also to his opponents, leaving himself fairly naked under his topcoat.

"You might as well take these, too," he said.

Without another word he proceeded outside and emptied his full bladder in the winner's gas tank which happened to belong to an expensive late-model La Salle.

Telling the story about himself years later, "Shake" would always grin, revealing a full set of matched pearly white false teeth mounted on what looked like candy wax dentures.

"I don't suppose they made it back to the Big Apple so easily with their winnings after that," he would say. "God help them."

George Travener
* *
*

Also called "George the Driver" because he was considered slow-witted but an excellent and safe chauffeur and road companion.

He never had a steady job, but was sometimes used by the well-to-do to ferry them to outlying places such as when the races were in session in Saratoga.

During Prohibition George drove for the bootleggers between here and Canada and made fairly large sums of money, but by then he was quite old, over seventy or even more.

His first wife had been shot and he held for the murder until the police found a more likely suspect in the person of a certain Bobineau, a Canadian.

Bobineau was a drifter. He was having an affair with the first Mrs. Travener, and with another Fort Edward woman who was asked to come forward and clear his name. But Bobineau was afraid to allow her to provide him with an alibi.

"She could say you were with her," his attorney said, pressing him for the woman's name.

The Frenchman said, "She might say I was not."

He was later executed.

That was in 1895 and, after that, Travener's life was rather uneventful, aside from the bootlegging. He drove a large Lincoln ambulance with hooch from

Rouses Point to The Hague and back regularly, and his sidekick was named Jesse.

He always wore a Stetson hat, and white and black Oxford shoes from Coward's.

He was a member of no lodge, and never was a churchgoer.

In the year after the Crash he married again, with a handsome local widow, Mrs. Harland, of fairly substantial wealth and property.

Their union lasted a full year before she succumbed to a senile dementia and had to be removed to the small county asylum at Argyle. George was very much in love with his second wife and, old and failing himself, agreed to move in with her where they co-existed another ten years behind straight jackets.

He was a strong man, standing well over six feet in height, and he was said to be the smoothest driver in the County.

His most characteristic expression was, "It makes a difference whose bull is gored."

Lorelei Dembitz
.
*

This small frail severe-looking woman with squinty grey eyes and very thin yellow hair had a high pale forehead.

Something waxy-looking about her face; it would spot with color around the cheeks when she would occasionally smile.

At the turn of the century Lorelei lived in a small frame house that had been in her family for nearly one hundred years. The large parcel of land surrounding it was listed as being in the village of Fort Edward, though she was very far from the small business district.

Lorelei was noted for two aspects of her life: she was employed as one of many County Clerks in the next-door town of Hudson Falls where she supervised the recording of all deeds, searches, and voting rolls; and she entertained this "very queer belief concerning her soul" which was articulated in a diary, found after her demise, that is preserved in the County archives.

Believing that her "soul" was not her own but that of another person, even smaller, frailer, and morally more "tattered" than she, Lorelei thought "this alien"—Francine, by name—had come to take possession of her sometime before her sixteenth birthday, when Francine was scarce fourteen. On bright sunny days, if she stood directly in the sun, "the shadow of this other can be seen hovering inside my own corporeal frame," she believed.

For that reason, Lorelei stayed much indoors except to go to and from her work. She had her groceries delivered and did not venture outside to garden herself but had a neighbor boy do it.

The embarrassment of having two souls distressed Lorelei. "I am most certain," she declared, "she and I do not converge throughout our entire integuments. If I lie down she extends somewhere between my shoulders and my knees. When I stand up she peers out through the nipples of my breasts. But we are not corollaries. She crowds my soul. She cramps my heart. I am not her coefficient."

It is perhaps strange that Lorelei did not confide her fears to any of the local physicians, but since she claimed that her "Francine" was a local girl who had been driven mad at fourteen (and she did not wish to be incarcerated as Francine had been inside her), that is somewhat understandable. She spoke to no one of her demon, and the thing grew fat inside her and flourished, like a cancer. Lorelei wrote: "Francine occupies me like an invader. I cannot post any part of my interior against her."

How she had come to be possessed was, she believed, a consequence of "accidental defloration" which, she averred, had commenced with the onset of the menses "during a pony ride with my late brother Simon."

To penetrate to the mystery of Lorelei's odd encrustation of beliefs and superstitions is to enter a very strange place indeed: she feared to take any medications when ill "that the imprisoned one might nauseate (?)"; and she would not take a boyfriend "fearing by mouth-kissing to spread this my contagion, for the alien could be sucked outside me into the person of my beloved." Although considered intelligent and efficient, Lorelei lacked for social activities. She was sometimes thought to be stand-offish, even unfriendly. "I am not much courted," she observed at age thirty. "Neither am I shunned. This that I am, inside who I am, tenanting me to aloneness."

The entering of one person into another is seldom without meaning, or without result, breeding at best children, at worst death: Lorelei, believing herself withal doubly cursed by the presence of her alien, sought to devise a sort of leasehold arrangement with her tenant which was never observed. The thing would not agree to stipulated dormancy periods; her appetites were voracious, her curiosities unlimited. It was as if the two made war inside a common amphitheatre like different corpuscles inside the blood. In one entry of more than fifteen pages Lorelei compares her vicissitudes to the action of "a spirit level."

> "Do I slip and slide? Hither and yon.
> As I go back and forth can I feel my center?
> My balance is to be all awobble. . . ."

She, as I say, did not confide this imagination concerning herself to any other person. Her diary, written in a tiny script, she willed to be preserved, but it was not to be perused until March 21, 1934, the hundredth anniversary of her birth.

What would happen to Francine upon her death? Presumably, "the mad one" would be liberated, as Lorelei stipulated that her remains should be made ready for preservation—but "no embalming fluids must enter my veins before the girl has been given time to escape."

She lived to be well over eighty, always, it seems, on her best behavior, as if by some mighty effort suppressing Francine inside her, and—as a consequence—seeming all the more empty and bland.

"That ectoplasmic sack inside my frame is ripped in places, tainted or tattered in others," she confided at age sixty, "and if it cannot be repaired except through my dissolution, then woe betide the person who may be possessed by it next, for it feels every rip and imperfection as the very texture of pain, and I am without any consolation save itself the alien and the potential for scandal which it breathes through me. Clearly I have been preoccupied of late. . . ."

Lorelei believed her constant migraines occurred because Francine's soul had crammed itself into her head.

She was often light-headed and dizzy, her feet a mess of pins and needles whenever "F deigns to lurk down there."

There are speculations in the diary about how F might go about relieving herself daily, about F's dietary requirements, and even if souls enter us naked, or clothed.

There was also the problem of communication between the alien and herself. Lorelei believed she had to move her lips silently to speak to the alien, and then she would always listen intently for any reply.

That she and Francine were regular attendants at the First Episcopal Church but "never once did she speak of her own person with Dr. Layden" was a matter of common discussion when her diary was inspected prematurely (against what she had expressly covenanted); and, then, too, there was much vile gossip about her fastidiousness of person, and the uncommon profusions of her gardens. But, during her lifetime, all observed a certain decorous silence concerning the lady. As she wrote: "This that vexes me insists I must be beyond reproach in every way, without any untoward blemish in the eyes of others. I go unnoticed to my liberation. . . ."

Although she continued to be single-minded about her work, Lorelei, aging, seemed to have difficulties concentrating on even the simplest tasks. She took an inordinate amount of time to answer rudimentary questions, and accomplish routine procedures.

Presently, the writing in the diary seems to come under the control of another hand. There are odd locutions, exclamations such as "stick figure" and "china doll" describing her innermost feelings of self-revulsion.

On January 6, 1903, she writes, "Francine has been unwell today and, as it is not my time, I know no relief by suffering for her."

The writing becomes oddly quirky: "She is in love . . . with him . . . God help us. Does he know it?"

"That she should be using me to be in his arms again tomorrow is appalling arrogance. That I cannot keep myself from cooperating indicates a certain lack of moral courage."

These entries all are made in reference to Victor Warren, a neighbor boy of eighteen who sometimes ran errands. He must have entered the lives of Lorelei-Francine sometime after her thirty-sixth birthday. Perhaps she truly found herself in love with this "young numbskull half my age," but she claimed it was Francine's crush.

In the voting rolls from 1922 on she listed herself as F. Lorelei Dembitz.

The last full entry is for April 23, 1924: "After all these years F. apologizes contritely for the confusing mess she has made of my life. She will do me no further harm. Snagged as I am. . . .

"My goal should be to recapture my life from this usurper.

"For the first time in forty years I can see, as if through my own eyes, an untroubled future. . . .

"Or perhaps she may also grow to like me and become my ally inside my body.

"Do I hate Francine? She despises her hostess.

"Lord save me from her spotty nightgowns!"

A month later she was found in "a state of entire neglect" and removed to the County Home at Argyle where she was to spend the rest of her life, languishing, without writing materials.

Her remains are buried in the Argyle Free Cemetery, and there is a second headstone beside her own that is inscribed, simply, FRANCINE.

Hetta Wessels
* *
*

Hetta Wessels was the daughter of an Army Colonel
(West Point, class of 1848) who perished at Antietam
in the War Between the States. When she was sixteen
her mother, Margaret, moved back from Fort Mead,
Virginia, to the family homestead just outside Lake
George on the Warrensburg Road. The great Insurrection was still raging; men were scarce; Hetta and
her mother did back-breaking labors of all sorts to
produce their livelihoods; and then, after about six
months, her mother arranged for her to become engaged to marry Warren Wessels, a farmer who had
only one hand and was, therefore, deferred. The wed-
ding took place in the Warrensburg Methodist church
and there was a collation afterwards at the Wessel
farm. Then the couple moved in with Warren's
mother. In the next three years Hetta produced two
girl children: Crystal and Estella.

In May 1867 Hetta became moody and disconso-
late. Crystal was three; Estella only ten months old:
her life was fast dwindling down to motherhood and
chores. She had been in a constant quarrel over the
past three years with her mother-in-law, Belle, and
found no pleasure in her marriage to Warren. One day
at breakfast he embraced little Crystal before going
out to his fields and told her, "I hope you never grow
up to be as ugly as your mother."

Yet the children fancied Warren more than her; they were his toys and playthings. Hetta merely cleaned them when they were dirty, and fed them when they were hungry; but it was Warren and Belle, that foul bitch, whom they adored.

That noon, after Belle went into Warrensburg to market, and Warren was still in his fields, Hetta prepared a creamy potato-and-leek soup for each of her babes and into each bowl she dropped a couple of large tablespoons of rat poison. When she was sure Crystal was no longer breathing she found her two largest traveling bags in the attic; into the larger of these bags she stuffed Crystal, and Estella into the smaller of the two. But the littlest child was still breathing faintly so she slammed the bag shut on her and stacked the larger bag containing Crystal on top of her.

Then she sat herself down at the kitchen table and composed the following note to Warren: "I am leaving you for good because, as you know, I do not love you. I hate you. I detest you. I cannot stand to sleep in the same bed as you. You do not know how to make me happy. You cannot make a woman happy in five minutes. You push and shove your filth in my face and you are a filthy bully, and now you are without your only loves."

Unfortunately, a neighbor woman dropped in then to borrow some coarse salt and, seeing the stout bags packed, and the note on the kitchen table, and the savage look in Hetta's eyes, she surmised the worst and summoned Warren from his fields.

Hetta tried to escape by running out the kitchen door to the corral. She hoped to steal one of her husband's horses, but she was apprehended even before she could mount. At first she would say nothing.

Then she said only that the "girls had gone off together, perhaps to pick wild berries."

By then Belle returned and discovered the note and the two cases with the girls' bodies. Warren threw himself on his wife and beat her savagely with his only hand, but the neighbor woman and Belle separated them, at last, and he was urged to take her in the wagon to the police in Warrensburg.

Hetta waited six weeks to be tried. In prison she was always quiet and well-behaved, calm, withdrawn, "neither gloomy or cheerful," as it was reported in the local press, "but as if she has taken sanctuary in prisoner's garb behind bars." But "she would speak of nothing of what had occurred at the farm except to admit she had been very unhappy."

She was put on trial for her life and her counsel required her to testify. Hetta called herself "the most unhappy woman in the world."

Then the judge inquired, "Have you never loved anybody?"

"I'm sorry to tell you that you must receive love in order to give it," was Hetta's reply.

"I am sorry to tell you," was the preface to everything she told the court. "I am sorry to tell you, your honor, I could not help myself. My father died; my mother was always sick and she cried a lot. Then I had to leave school in Virginia and come back here. The house was gloomy. I am sorry to tell you Mother did not wish me with her. I did not care for Warren. I am sorry to tell you that. He loved his mother more than me. They were a couple, Warren and his mother. I am sorry to tell you that. She made all the neighbors hate me. I had no friends, and I did not want my children to be as unhappy as their mother had always been. I am sorry to say, your honor, there was nothing else I could do. Suicide would have meant for me an eternity in hell. . . ."

Hetta Wessels was sentenced to death by hanging. Her sentence was never carried out.

Two nights before she was to die she choked on a hunk of bread in her cell.

Her jailors say her cell walls were covered with a three-word scrawl in Hetta's hand: "*I am sorry. I am sorry.*"

The Hargroves & Their
Farm Orchard
* *
*

The original Hargrove was Huguenot French. His arrival in the County in 1847 was also the signal for his dissolution. Octave was run over by a team of his own horses.

The wife and eldest son then purchased extensive acreage in the vicinity of South Argyle and cultivated their fields to grow European vines, a production for the tables of some local gentry.

A decent hock was made in large quantities under the family name, with a Huguenot Cross on the label; and a still champagne, and a fine cider, from all of which they prospered, eventually, through exportations to New York, New York, Philadelphia, and Boston; but their efforts were not greatly admired by our locals, many of whom were teetotalers, and, in 1863, a patriotic demonstration took place on their property during which all the Hargroves' barns, wine presses, fermentation vats, and oaken staved barrels were burned to cinders, with the suspicion being arson, and Miss Penelope Hargrove perished in that same fire, along with some livestock.

Then the young paterfamilias, Hypolite Hargrove, by now a husbander and father of three, rebuilt with the assistance of loans from New York, New York, but his vines suffered a blight and when expensive new vines would have to be imported from Burgundy or the Midi, he forswore the occupation of viniculturist, as such, and became interested in extracting the juices of certain local berries to produce numerous varietals of tasty fruit wines as a gastric aid.

For these a whole new product label was devised: *Dr. Hypolite's Fruit Tonics;* but again there was the Cross rampant, as it were, and he learned from some French cousins abroad how to infuse his tonics with quantities of cocaine, and they were now very popular among all manner of people. The orchards prospered, and a local custom for the tonics was established which more than offset the decline in sales of grape wines to the outlying city centers.

On every bottle Hypolite wrote in his own hand: "A fountain of youth in every bottle," and he signed each bottle with the name, Victor Hugo.

Now Dr. Hypolite's Fruit Tonics were said to be wonderful as a restorative for all manner of infirmities due to age and ill-health, and they were also administered as a daily tonic by farmers and their wives to withstand winter chills, and summer agues.

They were, it seems, a household word as far to the west as St. Louis, and were pronounced an excellent stimulant by no less than the Brothers Mayo, and Mark Twain.

Bottled in colored flasks that were shaped like military canteens, their colorful labels resplendent with fine illustrations of raspberries, blackberries, elder- and boysenberries, and cherries, they were even shipped abroad to Europe and South America, and one satisfied customer was the Mexican President Díaz.

All who suffered an ailment of some sort were

enjoined—through the written testimony of local physicians in Hypolite's employ—to use these fermented infusions to aid appetite failure, for the estoppal of flatulence, to cure depression and weak sexual coupling, to relieve the pain of arthritis, the gout, the heat of menopausal flashing, and insomnia.

Throughout the 1870s and 1880s Hypolite and his family prospered. He produced fifteen children and attributed his powers to his consumption of his own tonics. He took ads in the leading illustrated magazines, and got some of the leading artists of his day to endorse his fruit tonics, the likes of Nelly Melba, Jenny Lind, and Stracciatelli; all now found these did wonders for their breathing, and their vigor, during concerts.

In 1891 Hypolite, a millionaire, sold out to "New York interests" and moved with his family to the Southern tier where he would again produce vines for table wine.

But the new owners soon lost their custom and the orchards and extensive outbuildings and other holdings were sold to still other outlanders for a carriage factory, which eventually became a garage for automobiles.

In 1916, Matthew, eldest son of Hypolite and Agnes Hargrove, returned to Washington County briefly to propose to his childhood sweetheart, Elly Fulham.

She was engaged to a dairyman named Cobber.

Matthew took the trolley to Albany and, somewhere near Mechanicville, fell beneath its tracks and killed himself.

The other Hargroves have all perished; none presently lives in the County. Their orchard properties are in a state of neglect and abandonment, though locals occasionally come upon cases of the miraculous tonic in a shed that is still potable. But their place is still called Hargrove's Orchards, and always with an audible smacking of the lips by all.

The Artist Crow Marie, Painter
* *
*

Her paintings are all of the Upper Hudson valleys: small villages seized by light; patches of glassy water and sticky foliage, a shrub like fire, a toffee boulder, the red slicking of clay across a rutted country road after a rainstorm.

Like her earlier contemporary, Seneca Ray Stoddard, Crow Marie came originally to the Lake George region to paint scenics for the tourist trade, but she stayed on, built up a considerable local custom of her own, married with a local, a farmer, moved further south to a large brick house on the banks of the Canal at Northumberland, produced children, two girls and two boys, and did not personally turn to painting again until she was widowed in her middle forties and economic necessity drove her back to the palette and brushes.

Crow Marie was a handsome dark woman with a sharpish face, a large beaky nose, and close-cropped hair the color of slate. I knew the lady a little, having purchased a few of her smaller paintings for the family manse, and I was always glad to visit her at work, moved by her energy and hospitality, her care and wit, by the length and agility of her fingers, and the odd sour smells that seemed to cling to her smocks and the garments hiding that long ample body.

She was never really to be my friend, but I was considered a patron and fan, and she always insisted that the distinction prevail at all costs. When she was widowed a second time, I once offered her money. But she would only accept if I bought paintings from her, and when I did she threw in an extra for good measure, a pastel of the gloomy old family mill at Northumberland that lent the place an air of tragic mystery.

Her children, by then, were fully grown, and mostly away from the house. She had formed an alliance of sorts with a local "shadder," Black Neal, called simply Black, because he was, in part, his family hailing from Coon Box Hollow. But, if he lurked about her house at all times, we saw very little of him. Black drove a truck full of shad to market at Albany every day in spring, and sometimes he would come home drunk and sometimes he would call her names: "White bitch. White face. White whore and halfbreed!"

All this we learned much later from her children. Whenever I called, Crow Marie would make me coffee or tea, and show me her latest work. She always seemed very glad to see me, especially if I was of a mind to buy, and she resisted even my feeblest attempts at friendship, much less intimacy, howsoever cautiously put forward.

Then Black also took sick and died of the ptomaine infection, and she was alone again. I visited often, and not always with buying in mind. Crow Marie let me sit and watch her paint and I would help her with the miter box at making frames.

She would say little of her past even then except to tell me she was part Onandaga Indian, her father having worked the high steel, but she was more her mother's daughter, having been raised chiefly in New

York, New York, where the woman "took in men and was kept by them," in her words, "until she grew too old to attract the right sort and we lived in tenements "

Crow Marie said she had attended classes briefly at the Art Students League with Eilshemius and Glintenkamp. She had no family left of whom she spoke, other than that which she had produced, and no friends either. But, once, when I came to call, she was a long while in reaching the front door, and when she opened it, at last, to my surprise she wore a flowery red silk Japanese kimono that was partially unwrapped so that her shoulders and part of one rather full breast were visible. I was, of course, invited in while she excused herself to brush her hair and boil the water for tea. Crow Marie explained she had been working much too late at night, and overslept. But her face was very red and flushed, and I heard footsteps other than her own, and whisperings, in the back corridors of that large old house when she excused herself to dress.

Except to show her paintings to buyers, Crow Marie had very little contact with her neighbors, who were all mostly dairy farmers, or barge captains, and no very wide circle of acquaintances. "I live in here to look outside with my eyes," she would say, "and then I paint."

Crow Marie also said, "The fall is just colors to me. My eyes are canvas, and my flesh is getting like canvas, too."

She kept a large male cat called Jupiter and chickens for their eggs. She could play a slide trombone, and she was never ill. She did not seem to age as others; at sixty looking not much older than she had been at forty, nay, even handsomer.

When she had her seventieth birthday the children

and their spouses ran a party for her at the Queensbury Hotel and that included an exhibition of all her
latest work. Crow Marie came dressed in a long blue
velvet gown. She wore a white orchid in her hair with
ribbons of all colors, and she looked like some Polyne-
sian queen. The high moment of the affair came when
Crow Marie did a handstand to prove her agility and
her face was full of darkness as the blood rushed to her
head; she wore no underpants. Her pubic growth was
black and full, and her buttocks like pumpkins.

Afterwards, Crow Marie took a glass of champagne and sang:

> "My mother was an Indian whore
> and I am Crow Marie.
> Life is short and art is long
> and I am Crow Marie, the painter,
> and if some man shows me his root,
> I'll show him who will be the fainter."

She was much applauded, but only by some; her
children were among those who sat on their hands.
Yet there was not a painting left unsold.

Before next winter she sold the house, and moved
to a warmer climate: in Mexico where, I understand,
she thrived for quite a few more years with a companion who was also a painter, a Mex from the Art Insti-
tute at San Miguel Allende.

Then all her children moved to other parts, such as
Arizona and California, and nothing now survives her
having been here save for some paintings of the place,
and a collection of stereopticon photos she did with a
box camera and presented to the Hyde Museum.

There are some who would like to make her old
house in Northumberland into a historic landmark,
while others say: "She was not one of us. She was
Crow Marie."

Stace Coleman
& The Pessary Raid of 1886
.
* *

Stace Coleman was of an old County family. He counted among his immediate kinsmen Burns, Harlands, and Baskinds, and he was interconnected to the Ramsees who had colored among them.

Of no great wealth, save for land that was mostly rocky and just barely arable, it was only because of connections to some of the better County families that he was extended every sort of credit for his various business ventures.

Coleman was first a dairyman, and then a manufacturer of carriages. He failed at both these ventures, and went into jobbing of patent medicines and items for personal hygiene that were hard to find in the County. In a matter of three to five years he sold large quantities of "obstetric loungers," hot water bottles, and "galvanic appetizers," an electrical device connected to wet-cell batteries that sent electric charges through the liver designed to stimulate flagging appetites and sexual virility.

When the bottom fell out of our local economy in 1881, an outrage blamed on Jew bankers such as the Goulds and Fisks of metropolitan Gotham, Stace bought up large quantities of land and built houses; he also became a Notary Public and a publican. He owned and operated an inn in Eagle Bridge which he turned over to his sister, Hazel, and her husband, Sam, and a popular tavern on the Cambridge turnpike, and then, in 1887, swollen and engorged by such wealth, he returned to jobbing of a sort, becoming involved in a traffic in pessary sponges. This led to his brief arrest and imprisonment, for impairment of public morals, but again his ties to our great local familes served him in good stead.

Coleman was released and continued to pursue his contrabanding.

It should be recalled, in this connection, that the institution of birth control in or out of marriage was hardly known in much of Washington County at the time, or in the prospering lead and iron mines to the north, with any degree of formal arranging, until the years of the great Insurrection when, with so many men of family absent for so long a time, our local women required of themselves to devise, or have others devise, some means to protect themselves against unwanted generation, withal satisfying—to some degree—their needs as wives.

And when the men in blue returned they brought with them French letters, Dutch thimbles, various medicinal alums, and other such.

Nevertheless, chemical abortificants and instruments of abortion, hardly more sophisticated than the hat pin and coat hanger, were—alas—primary, even after the introduction from France by way of New York, New York, Savannah, and Charleston ports of the expensive lamb's-gut sheath; and many of my sex were either too ignorant or callous to care, and went about their husbandly tasks unprotected, like mariners who cast aside their slickers when they leave port, not knowing what storms may await them ten miles out to sea.

So it was that the introduction of the pessary, affixed to the cervical *os*, finally was to provide our local women with some protection against that most habitual infection to their wombs—increase.

Such women could be largely self-willed and self-fulfilled, even in our sternly Protestant precincts, but the tiny walnut-shaped sponges were not very easily acquired. The first were shipped South from British Canada, and they had to be doused in various alums and mild solutions of acid, and they were considered dangerous, if not outright immoral, by ministers and other guardians of public morality, including some local physicians.

In 1887, Stace Coleman, with his sister Conny, a spinster, having both faltered in their various efforts to obtain and increase the family wealth, thought of taking a large trading sloop down the Champlain Canal to New York, New York, and from thence out into the open sea where they would endeavor to rendezvous off the coast of the Bermudas with the French brigantine trawler, *Aréthuse*, that was loaded to the gunnels with sponges from Sint Maarten and the Dry Tortugas.

With the industry of some fifty local boys (recruited because they were undersized and would not greatly increase the weight and bulk of their cargo), Coleman hoped to be able to manufacture aboardships on the return voyage many thousands of these pod-shaped objects, and from thence, sailing back along the canal and employing some pretty country matrons to be his salespersons, he would quite literally hawk and market his infamous wares from door to door until he had even passed north of all the villages on our great inland sea, where the remainder would be traded in Burlington, Vermont, to Canada and New England.

All proceeded apace until it came time to affect that predestined rendezvous in rather high seas during a storm off the coast of what is now called Elbow Beach when his precious cargo was spilled overboard and three of his boys lost to the voracious sea. Bankrupt, and disgraced, Stace Coleman returned to the County empty-handed. But, again, no pressure was brought on him to make reparations, as the boys had all been homeless waifs, and also because of his good connections.

Coleman, moreover, was not for very long discouraged. He borrowed money from some and sold shares to others and now it even happened that he was able to secure the transfer of his goods from one deck to the other when his party sailing north, just beyond the shoals of the Golden Isles of the Carolinas (and preoccupied with their manufacturing upon the forecastle) stopped to replenish their water casks in some tributary of the Ashley River and were boarded by a party of privateering former Confederates, their treasure denied them, their sloop put to the torch, and all just barely escaping with their lives.

All this I know from my own paternal grandma who remained on friendly terms with Stace, despite all. As a token of that amity he gave her one of the few devices he was able to salvage from his second voyage, which she told me she used for nearly twenty years to good effect. She even produced the thing for my inspection and it was not only walnut-shaped, but walnut-hard.

Grandmother Spyker also told that Stace Coleman, much discouraged, returned to a farmhouse he had purchased, previously, outside Whitehall, and raised bees, and minks for their fur, and married with the only prominent local suffragette, Penny Bronkhurst, but was not much heard from in a public way for nearly twenty years when he ran for the State Legislature as a "greenbacker" and a "dietist" and was easily defeated, and shortly thereafter died.

As Grandma put it to me, "He was a man ahead of his time, that Stace, including all his bankruptcies, and even when we didn't respect him we were all a little in awe of his adventuresome nature and rather carefree set of ideas."

A further word about the Ramsees who I mentioned earlier as being "of color." I take my authority, again, from Grandma Spyker who claimed they once all lived in Coon Box Hollow. She said Jed worked in the Sandy Hill Post Office and was "as white as any man among us, to look at, though he was a 'kinker'."

She said they were all much loved and respected, and nobody ever denied them their voice in the community, Ralph Ramsee even working in our family mill for the same wages as any other able-bodied man.

It was this same Ralph Ramsee, coincidentally, who later married with Stace Coleman's sister, Conny, when she was past the age of childbearing and they adopted many homeless youths and raised them as Christians, among them one of our recent mayors.

And some people claim Ralph also fathered many children who still walk our streets as adults, once he and his left the Coon Box Hollow, and that he was called by his peers "a man who can" because he really could, but some of this is, no doubt, just gossip and malice, and backbite.

Stace Coleman and Ralph Ramsee became close

friends after the debacle of 1887 and the subsequent marriage to the sister, and Grandma Spyker swore Ralph was often heard to say he thanked Providence for those privateers who had, in their way, delivered unto him the hand of Conny Coleman.

Austin Flint,
"The Virginia Buck"
* *
*

Came to South Argyle, allegedly from Roanoke, Virginia, in 1891, to pursue a career in pulp.

Married in 1895 to Mary Winslow, school mistress.

1896, Onslow Flint.

1897, Arnot Flint.

1899, Dunster Flint.

1901, Aiken Flint.

There was also a stillborn of the union in 1900 and again in 1902, but none were girls.

From 1899 to 1912 Austin Flint presided over the Unified Unitarian Congregation of Washington & Warren Counties.

Chased from his pulpit in 1912 for "numerous fornications and vilenesses perpetrated against his parishioners."

Purchased "Dead Farm" on Dutchtown Road in 1912 and sought to make his living raising miniature beef cattle "such as could be slaughtered for a family's needs without undue waste."

Filed for bankruptcy in August 1914.

Purchased *The Town Crier News* in 1915 to serve the areas of Greenwich, Middle Falls, Lake Cossayuna, and South Argyle.

Bankruptcy, 1915.

1917, removed himself to New York City to avoid his various creditors and was never heard from again.

Flint's only surviving memorial in Washington County being his nickname, "Virginia Buck," which to this day is used to refer to a randy gentleman of delicate manners "who does not observe that most difficult of Commandments fastidiously."

The Lickworm Chronicle
* *
 *

A fellow over to Middle Falls, or Grangerville, started raising lickworms to provide his household with provender: what you call night crawlers.

His name was Daniel Deloache. He was a Frenchy, and the people would stop and buy from a roadside stand, all spring and summer, and into the fall, mostly trout fishermen, but some perchers, and ice fishers.

He claimed to grow some "very tasty worms."

He was a brawny man with freckles and a lot of carrot red hair and so were his kids.

They all seemed fine, and were getting by, and there were a number of wrecked Chevvies behind the house, and a VW bus in pretty good shape, and a Ford pickup.

People said Deloache knew how to raise good bait.

There were three kids, in all, I believe, and the youngest was maybe six when he started going to school with other children, on the bus, and that's when the trouble started, at the hot lunch, over a plate of Franco-American spaghetti. When the kid saw his bowl overflowing with spaghettis and sauce, he very calmly told all the other kids they ate worms just like that at home, only not with tomatoes: maybe just some turnips, or parsnips, stewed in.

He wasn't complaining. He said it was good; and it turned out he'd never seen spaghetti before.

But, he said, the worms at home were just a little different, thinner. He referred to what was in his bowl as "blood worms."

Well, he was disciplined for upsetting all the other children with his nonsense, and causing a number of the girls, and quite a few boys, to throw up all over themselves, and when he was brought to the principal's office it turned out he had not been fooling anybody.

Deloache was called to school, and he denied everything. Gave the boy an angry and cross look as if to box his ear.

Then some people said the matter was settled—except it wasn't. Mrs. Deloache got in a rage at her old man a few weeks later and told all: how she and Deloache sometimes ate sidebacon and a smoked butt with greens, or a kidney, but the boys were fed only worms at Deloache's insistence and told this was spaghetti.

They were all summoned to the clinic in Cambridge and examined, and seemed in good fettle, and then the Society for the Prevention of Cruelty got interested in the matter through the papers, and they went to court, and sued, to place the children in foster homes.

A very strange and curious affair, if I must say so. Can't really recall if those kids were ever placed; but I've always called them lickworms ever since, because, you know, when that oldest boy, Howard, was asked what a worm tasted like, he confessed he had never tasted any because he just never had the inclination or the time. "I just licked 'em," he explained, "and slurped 'em down before I started to gag. . . ."

Was there no other food or condiment served the children of the Deloache household? he was asked.

Howard replied that every couple of weeks his ma made them all chop suey, mostly on Sunday nights.

Hardiman Roc

* *
*

A pedlar by trade, he is best known for his Prawn connection, by marriage, and also for his tradesman's chant which became the delight of schoolchildren:

> "Delight in me ladies
> I bring you bright threads,
> buttons and snaps,
> and skeins of new wool.
> I have more in my store,
> but my pack is quite full."

He gave cash for old clothes, too, and would sing,

> "For your old clothes
> I give cash
> such as nobody knows,"

to the tune, approximately, of *The Star-Spangled Banner*.

He was a lonely bachelor, born in County Galway, Ireland, until his thirties when he made a common-law arrangement with Ann Roc (no relation).

He continued to peddle and they produced two offspring: Bonita and Maybel.

They purchased a general store in South Argyle but he continued to peddle, growing restless with the sedentary commercial life.

The farmers liked him because he gave credit, always writing down the sums owed in a small black school-exercise book, and never pestering until after the harvest.

At the Saratoga Racing Meet in 1903 he encountered Sarah Gainham who called herself a seamstress. Since her address was in New York, New York, they removed themselves there, and were never heard from again until their deaths, by asphyxiation, in a tenement in the Hell's Kitchen.

Ann Roc's Maybel had married with Berthell, who ran a steam excursion boat on Lake Luzerne. Then she herself made another connection, with a joiner. She purchased a rooming house, and found a suitable mate for Bonita in the slow-witted son of the Borgs.

All in all, a strong and remarkable woman who, when she learned of Hardiman's demise, felt badly (though she was now a Dolfussy). "My poor packman has neglected to shut off the little gas nipple and perished with a lady," she lamented. "Were he not so neglectful he might have written us sooner, or sent a telegram, that we would not be seeing his likes again until The Great Reunion."

She purchased no headstone for him in the County, but had Maybel's first son named Hardy in his honor, and when she married a third time, late in life, to the Jew (or Arab?) storekeep Baziote (we never knew for sure), she still spoke well of Hardiman to her new class of friends.

Serendipity Flatch

* *
   *

It is not always honestly given, but you will have a better time, nevertheless, if, when a woman loves you, you take that love seriously.

Such will not always be lasting, and may not continually please; but, while it does, that is the sweetness of life. If you once deny it of any woman, moreover, for the time you do your life will be a bitterness, and a misery, and you will have only yourself to blame, whereas if you allow them to love you as they say they do, and respond, be chosen and admired, it is always a flattery; and you can blame them for the neglect, when it occurs, and for the loss of love, if it so happens.

This advice, random and abstract as it may seem, is inspired not simply by any desire I may have to recall a lifetime of pleasure and dissipation as my days on earth grow shorter; it is also inspired by the story of Serena Flatch, who, in her terms, was a much wronged woman.

The Flatches were a family of wealthy Dutch farmers from Friesland who settled the area around Victory Mills sometime in the 1840s. The name, which is a Holland corruption of Fletcher, suggests early English antecedents. Serena was their third child, and only daughter, "very beautiful and shapely of loin and thigh," with a high coloring and pert elegant features, according to her photos.

But she was hardly serene. She was considered very flighty as a young girl and fanciful and imaginative, subject to odd fancies, and crushes, and wayward about obedience. In 1854 she was caused to marry a Dusinberry and moved to Sandy Hill. Since Dusinberries were intermarried with Harlands, and Brinks, there was considerable wealth and ease in that family. Serena's husband, T. Rex, never worked but lived off family shares in a mill and a glove factory. He was said to be "not very much as men went," and spent many years studying the habits of migratory loons.

Bored with her husband's preoccupations, Serena tried to win him over by her amorous interests, but he was not much interested. Then she grew very cross and took lovers, never bothering to hide her shame. Serena became a voluptuary and a debauchee, a wanton, a hussy, a harlot, no better than the meanest lowest country wench. In short, a woman scorned, etc.

In seven years she bore him five children; they were by, at least, three different men, aside from T. Rex, who abandoned sleeping with her entirely. Then, nothing, not even the demands of motherhood, could distract her from her waywardness and wantonness; and she took women lovers as well, and began to flaunt herself about town, smoking Havana cheroots, with parties of sporting men and women.

Still, T. Rex was withdrawn and would show no interest in her.

Still, she confessed an injured love for him, and a contempt, almost, as it were, in one and the same breath.

Serena became, consequently, a predator; no honest woman's husband, or betrothed, was safe from her depredations.

They called her a "powerful great whore" and "the black hole of Calcutta." Still, they were seduced by her blandishments, and easiness.

She caused to have built a shack in the woods near Moreau where she would sometimes retire for days at a time with her latest conquest, and there were orgies, too, and, always, upon her return, T. Rex was informed, or she would pretend to this gullible ass that she had merely been to New York, New York, on a shopping trip.

Serena was so fearsomely beautiful, and so openly gay and flirtatious, that her shamelessness was not without charm: she had hair like a dark flame rising high above her head, and her breasts were as ample and full as if they had been scooped from the hills of Carrara.

She never denied any willing man any thing, including what she called love, and she was much sought-after.

Presently, her Lupercalian activities in the woods attracted public notice and she was forced to separate from T. Rex and remove herself and her babes to Schenectady where she opened a shop for women (a sort of high-fashion boutique for the sporting element); and then she hired lawyers to divorce herself from Dusinberry with his consent for a price; her scandalous grounds being "impotence."

But the other members of the Dusinberry clan wished to forestall this scandal, and when one of T. Rex's brothers came to see her to plead his case (and that T. Rex might be allowed to see his brood of children) she seduced the brother, too, who came to be a member of her sporting party, when she had dismissed him as her lover.

Likewise, her husband's lawyer, Leary Clark, was seduced, and Eastwood, the mayor, and even various of the clergy who attempted to intercede; and there were rumors about her and her eldest son, a striking handsome boy of fifteen called Tic, though his full name was Tice.

By now Serena was pregnant again, and nobody knew by whom (and some feared by the boy, her son). She was prevailed upon to return to her family, but her behavior there was so entirely lewd she soon had them scandalized, too, and she was asked to pack her things, and a small settlement was made on her.

Serena used the money to purchase a large house in Fort Ann, quite near to the center of the village, and this she converted to an inn of sorts, or place of accommodation (for the purpose of rendezvous), and she served refreshments of all sorts to those on the stagecoach route to Lake Champlain. What a pity that her reputation had preceded her to this new place, for she was accorded no good welcome by her Fort Ann neighbors, ever.

Finally, she took an Indian for lover and she and he together succumbed to a bleary life of alcohol, jimson weed, and other vices.

A wasted life, for one so beautiful. . . .

In retrospect, Serena has been hailed by some of our younger generation of Sandy Hill females as an early Washington County feminist, a sort of George Sand without novels, but that is to blur distinction's visage: The virago was spurned, so she lived in voluptuary flames and finally perished in the ash and cinders of her passions; but she was no more likely a supporter of Suffragettism than she was of Vegetarianism. Serena's only interests were to pleasure and be pleasured. She was a true slut, befouling the institutions of motherhood and marriage. She was the despite of property, respectability's monster, and when she took me to bed with her in her sixties at the inn in Fort Ann I enjoyed great delight; for she was still fantastically beautiful, and agile, and playful, and she taught me much about the ways of a woman, so that for years afterward I always referred to her as my "Madame Professor."

Serena is buried in Fort Edward. I had her buried and paid for the tombstone. The inscription is one of my own verses:

> "Her skin was red.
> She took to bed
> a red-skinned knave
> who was her slave.
> Passionate sporter,
> this Dutchman's daughter,
> forsaking breath,
> has entered death.
>
> R. I. P. Serena."

Brewer Ochs

* *
*

Ernest Ochs was a brewer, wealthy, of Fort Edward. He was known to be generous and fat.

One day a man with a sallow complexion called on Brewer Ochs and told him that his former father-in-law, John Lehnert, had been injured in Saratoga and was anxious to have him come to him without alarming the family.

Mr. Ochs boarded a trolley car with the stranger and rode to Saratoga in front of the United States Hotel where they alighted. They then walked to a one-story shanty which stood a hundred yards from the nearest house.

The stranger led the way into the house and, pointing to an inner room, the door of which was closed, said: "He's in there."

Mr. Ochs started to enter the room, but as he opened the door he caught sight of a heavily built man in his stocking feet, who tried to jump behind the door. The other man pressed close behind Mr. Ochs and tried to force him into the room.

Then it flashed through the brewer's mind that he had been trapped by confederates of "Boiley Yam," or worse.

Mr. Ochs, who had a brewer's muscled girth, turned quickly and pushed the fellow behind him aside, and ran out of the place. He ran to the nearest house and gave an alarm.

Constable Behlen, in company with several other men, proceeded to the shanty, but found it locked. The door was forced open, and several pieces of rope tied in a noose were found. There was also an open trap door, and beside it a pick handle. No one in the vicinity knew the strangers who had been seen about the neighborhood for several days. But it was speculated that the motive was simple robbery, as Mr. Ochs had considerable valuable jewelry about him, and also a large sum of money.

Mr. Ochs was a bachelor widower. He returned home to Fort Edward only to discover that the thieves' confederates had emptied his house (through the door he had left ajar in racing to the aid of Lehnert) of furniture, plate, his dead wife's furs, and jewels, and three large hogsheads of Fort Edward beer.

Walter H. Foley

* *
*

In Sandy Hill, or near, there was for a time, on one of the bluffs overlooking our great Hudson, a small mine for the extraction of yellow ochre and kaolin. This ochre, yellow or burnt red, was used to make pigments, and paint, and dyes for the wallpaper factory nearby; and the kaolin formed into clays of all sorts. Walter H. Foley, for a short while, also used that substance for a patent medicine he called "Honey and Tar."

The tar in this case being kaolin, it was advertised to "cure colds, prevent pneumonia." Foley also made a Blood Bitters with the leaves of certain local burdock plants, "guaranteed to cure the national ailment which is Dyspepsia," and an infusion of "sweet fern in boiled spring water" which was believed to "cure the itch and pain of poison ivy poisoning."

An interesting man, who came here from Pulaski to the northwest where he had produced a "laxative fruit syrup" that received good references from, among others, Chas. J. Dodge, and Surrogate C.I. Miller, he married with a local woman, dissolved his previous company, and moved here. For a while, he prospered, too, in a large house near Fort Miller, with outbuildings that distilled his products, including something called "Australian Leaf," a "herb cure for women's ills," said to have been discovered by a New York nurse of good repute originally from the outback. Foley kept a diary, and it is preserved, wherein he notes using the local kaolin to invent "a sanitary corn pad," and a "regulate" that was both "pleasant and aromatic."

He seems to have been much preoccupied with his health, and that of others. On January 4, 1908, he writes: "I have been somewhat costive. Got just the results required with my Regulator. . . ."

On February 10 we learn: "Backache, kidney, bladder, and urinary troubles. I shall try my Butternut Balsam."

Again on March 3: "To promote flow of digestive juices prepared a salad of fresh burdock leaves. Stomach membranes considerably strengthened."

We do not know if he was as assiduous in caring for the health of his wife Sally with such homegrown remedies, but we do know he evolved a curious system of notations to record every instance in which they engaged in acts of marital love. Foley marked his diaries with an (!) to indicate that both had been pleasured, whereas a (?) indicated only his own satisfaction. In one entry, running for several pages during the year 1910, we read: "Sally much preoccupied of late with acts of preservation and I do not challenge her except once (?) and early the next morning she is somewhat more talkative (!) and then, at luncheon, after cold meat and pickles (!?), so that I have begun to wonder what to make of her except as my helpmate and the source of my most excruciating pleasures. We went to town later and on the way back in the wagon she and I were ****(?), but it was good all around, she averred. . . ."

Foley came out for temperance earlier than some,

citing the grim statistics of declining Leavenworth, Atchison, and Pittsburg, Kansas, where drink was openly dispensed, as opposed to prosperous Kansas City, in a letter to the papers, and then he ran for the legislature and was defeated. He did not quaver in his despisal of strong drink, which he believed caused cancer, and in the year 1910 placed a small advertisement in papers throughout the State:

CANCER CURED
TO STAY CURED
without pain, inconvenience, or leaving home
NO KNIFE—NO PLASTER—NO PAIN

It was recommended that interested parties were to write to a certain post-office box in Kingsbury if they wanted details, but the takers never met the costs of such publicity, and Foley, eventually, had to file for bankruptcy.

He died a few days before the assassination at Sarajevo and his diary records: "!!!! I cannot believe our current disarray. What has been happening about this place bodes ill for all: Gross exhibitions, licentiate buffoonery, abandonment to the vicious, it is as if behind these doors lies Sodom, or some seminary of vice. . . ."

Foley left no heirs. His wife sold off their holdings and soon left the County.

His only memorial, other than what he wrote, is found on the walls of an old brick building I passed once out to the west near Gowanda, an advertisement for a certain "FOLEY'S ELECTRICAL OIL" which, I am pretty sure, was another of his concoctions, as the large white letters on the side of the old Flemish brick house averred, "A liniment for cold and coughs. Prevents hemorrhages. You'll wake up sound as a bullet."

Cack The Sissy

* *
*

Born in a pesthole, sired by a lout and a jade, and treated most cruelly by both throughout his childhood, Cack the Sissy grew up in our midst to wear his nickname of opprobrium like a war decoration.

He never went to schools, and could neither read nor write.

He was ill-housed, and ill-fed, and sometimes was forced to wear women's clothes to keep his frail body warm.

He was known to relieve himself in the church pews, and he pestered some of the little boys.

Great sport was made of Cack by others: he was called "jack-o'-lantern face" and "moon boy," "twit" and "girly."

Once he was taken in by a farmer on the Vaughn Road to do chores, but the man lost patience with his squeamishness, and filthy traits.

He finally found work at the Hercules plant, but fell (or was pushed) into a vat of fulminate and dissolved almost to the bone.

Pointer

* *
*

Pointer was no cur, but he might as well have been for the treatment he received from all; and nobody knew why.

He had no kin, and seemed to have wandered into our town from elsewhere, calling himself simply Pointer.

He took work on the sleeping-car siding of the D & H railway, making up berths for the New York trains at night.

He slept beneath a caboose, they say, in a blanket roll, well into the winter, when he removed himself to an old mine shaft near Moreau.

He had no friends.

He was a passable good shot with a .22 or a pellet gun, and because he was one-eyed some speculated he had seen service, in the Indian wars, or with the Grand Army of the Republic during our Great Revolt.

He could recite to anybody who was interested most of Lincoln's Second Inaugural Address, and Othello's speech to the Venetians after strangling Desdemona about that "circumcised dog."

We never saw much of him after the Flu Epidemic in '19 and in 1926 a skeleton was found in the woods near Moreau by picknickers that many swore was Pointer.

Norman Paige

* *
  *

Originally from way upstate near Malone. An educator, but barely educated himself, he coached basketball, and taught Algebra at Fort Edward High when I was a boy and was there until only a few years ago when he retired, and, shortly thereafter, died.

He had a queer habit of using only fine linen hankies with his initials in blue and drying them out on the school radiators during class. They made an odd crackling sizzle, not unlike frying.

He must have had stock in Stewart's Ice Cream, for he ate so much of it, particularly their cherry vanilla.

He wore suits with vests of a thick utility grade tweed and herringbone, mostly all grey, and little black garters on his sleeves.

Once he taught History and confused the Emperor Maximilian with Metternich, and he was taken up on it by Arnold Benjamin who had a brain for that sort of thing.

He was certainly no historian, but he didn't do a heck of a lot better with Algebra, or basketball, except that people felt sorry for him.

He claimed to know some famous people such as a man named Harry Stack Sullivan, a doctor famous like the Mayo Brothers, with whom he had grown up near Malone, and the man who invented Kleenex, and the Scheins.

He could play a clarinet.

Favorite expression: "Hand me that melon."

Newton Pruyn

* *
 *

No relation to the lumbering and paper baronetcy, he was a poor Pruyn, or, as we used to say, a Prune.

Took a degree in ceramic engineering at Alfred and wound up designing burial crypts and vaults.

Married Heather Mayall, Canuck, and two kids. Divorced, and married an Usteban girl, from Austerlitz, or Petersburg, I forget which.

Settled for a while in Williamstown, Massachusetts, and then North Adams, before coming back north where he got into drain pipes and conduits. Stuff of that sort.

Not a really noteworthy life, but worth noting anyway for a degree of ingenuity, and his imaginative grasp of the possible, as he was eulogized last spring.

I never knew what his favorite expression was. The only thing I ever heard him say tell was, "Bullshit." Stuff like that.

He was just pretty bitter about losing his kids, and he was born with two strikes in his mouth in this town, having a name like Pruyn.

His son Ned was one of the organizers of the Battle of Schuylerville that was staged for the Bicentennial.

Married somebody related to those Carvel people: Greek Jews, Levrac.

Lives in Florida, or maybe Arizona.

Chester Bowles

* *
 *

It has not been my purpose to write of the many workingmen who have been employed for decades at General Electric, or Hercules Powder, behind lathes, on packing benches, or at the wheel of drill presses, or ladling from the great vats, for they are largely of a class and of a background of which I know little: They labor for wages, fraternize through their unions and other associations, and when we chance to meet in bars, on the streets, or during one of my occasional visits to the VFW, we are hardly better known to each other than strangers, though our paths may have crossed hundreds of times before, and we have been neighbored for decades, too.

But there are certain exceptions to my claim of ignorance of the working classes of Sandy Hill and vicinity and of these I should like to take some notice: of Chester Bowles, for example, who was a name to me before he ever was a face, or figure. I heard of him first shortly after I returned from the war in Europe. My friend Erny Trueshank was organizing a party for deer hunting in the woods near Moreau where he had this camp, and he said Ben DaVinci and Chester Bowles would be going along and did I care to come too?

I was not much for hunting but in those days I was a bit of an *arriviste* and the opportunity to meet so distinguished a businessman and statesman as the late Chester Bowles (even though I have always voted GOP) was intriguing to me.

"I didn't know he had a place in the County," I told True: "*The* Chester Bowles . . . ?"

"The very same," he said.

"And you know him?" I inquired. "You socialize?"

"With all you younger fellas gone for the war," said True, "there wasn't much else I could do."

And he shrugged, sadly.

"I would very much like to meet him sometime," I explained, "but not hunting, I think . . ."

"Anytime you like," True said.

"How?"

"We could just drop by and have a drink with him sometime," said True. "Chester, he really likes visitors."

To make a long story short, we went that very afternoon to a shabby-looking farm house in the Moreau woods and were greeted by an aged old coot with a caved-in face wearing old grey baggy railway trousers and red striped gaiters, and he was *the* Chester Bowles, but the *wrong* Chester Bowles. This Chester Bowles was a retired D & H railway engineer, and I had to stay and chat for two hours about the condition of the rails between here and Mechanicville, and we all got very soused on homemade dandelion brandy before True made his excuse for both of us, and we were free to take our leave of Chester Bowles.

Afterwards, in True's big blue Packard he asked me, "Well, what did you think of Chester? How did you like him?"

"He wasn't quite the go-getter I expected," said I.

Teach me to social climb.

Brody Shansky

Brody Shansky was a mick neighbor I had for a while
when I lived off Mohican Terrace not very far from the
Boulevard.

He worked at the G.E., first as a packer, later a
dipper, but he lost three fingers and part of his nose in
the acids somehow and I don't think he worked much
at all when I knew him.

There are three things I can tell you for certain
about Brody Shansky:

1. He had only two pair of underpants and did his
wash every day, winter or summer: the same two pair
of briefs with elastic waistbands. Same spots in peculiar places.

2. He read *The Sporting News* every week and
saved all the papers in a shed near his back porch that
caught fire the summer the boys went off to Korea,
and then he kept the papers on the porch, until the day
he died, I guess, piled up higher and higher.

3. His favorite food was bacon. You couldn't mis-
take the smell of it so thick and greasy in our alley I
almost slid on the fat of it whenever I carried out
garbage cans.

He had a hunting dog bitch, name of Sarah, and
had never married, and never hunted.

He played pinochle and punch once a week at the
VFW.

He hated Harry Truman, and Dennis James, the wrestling announcer, equally, though I know not why.

He liked to talk headlines with you Sunday after lunch, but in his case it was always about Truman who he would call corrupt, a nigger-lover, and a jackass. "I'm from Missouri. Show me," he would always say, if you argued with him.

He was once caught molesting a neighbor woman late at night with a pitchfork and sickle through her bedroom window, and was taken away to the Mental Health Center in Glens Falls for a few days, but then they released him and he moved back into his house, and kept pretty much to himself until the day I moved away. He wasn't really any pervert, I think, just a lonely grouchy old man with his disfigurements. He told the neighbor woman he wanted her to "help him out with a little problem he'd been having lately . . . a certain weightiness he'd been feeling in the legs. . . ."

When he was in the hospital his married daughter Peggy, who married the Witness, told me her father had his money buried somewhere in the backyard.

I doubt that.

Nobody puts away very much working at the G.E.

P.C.B. Terry

* *
*

The name was Terrazini. The initials stand for a chemical used at the G.E. where he worked. He'd swallowed a mouthful once from what he took to be the water jug. Terry's real first name was Paul, as I recall, and I don't know if the rest ever meant anything much. Well, with all that slow-acting poison in his system, they retired P.C.B. on the disability compensation and he spent the years he had left growing and canning Italian tomatoes. He must have grown two or three acres solid with tomatoes every season, and they were a sight to behold: a mess of red in the backyard of his house, which abutted mine in Fort Edward, though he was the only guy who ever ate any of them, he and maybe his wife. P.C.B. couldn't give those tomatoes away though they were all pretty to look at, and put up in nice Ball jars, too, for the winter, for sauces, and spaghettis. The trouble was, most people were afraid of getting his poisons. It wasn't likely possible, not from eating tomatoes, but the superstition persisted, and only people like yours truly used to take and store the jars in his cellar with a proper "thank you" to P.C.B. Most other folks were outright rude to him. They would ask, "What's going on here? What are you up to, P.C.?" Or, "Hell, no . . . !" Still, he grew them and bottled them and offered them stewed or in their natural state to whomever he could. And the wife would wink and encourage him. Really egg him on.

By the time P.C.B. died I had over one hundred jars in my basement unused. Then I thought to get rid of them but how. You just couldn't dump them any old place in the landfill. The seepage. And what if the birds or other mice got into them? I finally hired a truck and drove them across the river to Moreau and they were buried in a pit underground where they will never be found, I hope.

P.C.B. had a marvelous humor about his affliction, too. When there were floods in the Berkshires and Northern Connecticut in the Fifties and a lot of people were left destitute he offered to contribute over five thousand jars of tomatoes he had put up, and the offer was gratefully declined by the officials at the Red Feather who explained to P.C.B. the problems of shipping.

His favorite expression was, as I recall: "It don't matter where it goes in, it's gotta come out somewhere, too."

Alf Legerman

* *
 *

Here was a sturdy fellow, a master mechanic, handsome as a piece of oak dresser, and sturdy. Nobody ever had a bad word to say about him. He was the match for any man in thinking, too. He worked at the G.E. until he had a grubstake and then went into dairy farming. Then he had to go back to the G.E. or lose his farm. They made him a production foreman. The Communists had a union they were trying to get sanctioned from the men, and Alf said he wanted to be represented too and went back to the line. Then he lost a foot somehow in a freak accident, and then he lost his farm. Last I heard he did some part-time security work for the toilet-paper mill in Greenwich.

Landis James

* *
 *

He once ran for Mayor of Glens Falls as a Socialist. I doubt he got ten votes. Times were good and in those days the Falls was as fine a small business city as you can find anywhere, even sort of progressive. Now it's all malls, and blight in the center of town, like a mouth missing teeth. I thought Landis James had moved away long ago but I saw him only a few weeks back at the Washington County Fair. He had a pair of beasts entered in the oxen pull and seemed preoccupied, and, as you would expect, a lot older and wiser. His wife was selling frozen cider in plastic jugs, and he told me he had an Agway franchise in Battenville.

A funny sort of a man, I think, even for Washington County. He had this friend from New York, a gentleman farmer and a swell, with a big spread out near Greenwich, and the two once tried to put out a local paper. They called it *The Weekly People.* By the time of their second issue they'd run out of capital and were a bit stretched for credit. They were calling themselves "Jeffersonians" in those days. Frankly, I'm a bit sorry Landis James never caught on in the County with any of his political ideas: he came from an old County family, the Jameses, up above Hartford, and he was a wonderful public speaker. Some people said the best they'd ever heard anywhere, including those who could remember T.R. and Bryan. But I don't think you could sell Socialism in Washington County even in hard times.

Landis had a brother, Gaynor. He was said to be very good with women, and knew a lot about mushrooms.

There was a sister, too, but she passed away around the time of the influenza epidemic in New York.

Marie Amboyster
(also called Marie The Witness)
* *
*

There was a woman for you, radical as hell with her ideas for the women of the County, but she never caught on either, and then she saw the light and became a Jehovah's Witness and opened up a Laundromat.

When I first knew her she was all for Birth Control and Suffrage. A nice woman, with a comely face, and brains too. She had a lot of beaus: even a major-league baseball player from the Giants: Hal Trotsky, I think that was his name. He was no slouch. Played the infield and pitched the knuckle ball some, too.

Well, she was a free soul in those days and scandal would have easily attached to her name except that she was the best seamstress they ever had and there was just no way you could put her down because she had skills.

People just didn't care that much about the other stuff if you helped them to make more money.

I would have courted her myself, if not for Mother and her pretensions.

I believe she wanted to be a great lawyer some-day, and she took stenography courses and worked for one of the firms for a while, but nobody ever encouraged her to go any farther so she left and went back to her sewing machine, and then she met this guy Worthheimer, a Witness, and something must have happened because she was one of them, too, after a little while, and then they opened up their Laundromat, and they keep pretty much to themselves, the Witnesses, like a lot of people in Sandy Hill, only maybe more so. Now what I will never understand is why we allow people to waste themselves like that. She could have been something. Her sister married a doctor, but he was a Jew. Still, people liked him. And used him.

It's a funny place, the County. People say not much has really changed. But an awful lot has, I assure you. Not many like me are left anymore. The place isn't just going to the dogs. It's sprinting there next Sunday at Green Mountain, and maybe that's the better for some people, but not for me.

Still and all, it's a place like any other place and I suppose it doesn't really matter. None of it. The important things remain the same and we'll all be dirty dust someday, and dead.

I get a laugh at the radicals who think any differently. A few years back, this bloke sent me a magazine from New York, New York, about some group of insurrectionists who were causing a lot of trouble to the Rockefellers, and others, downstate. It was said in this publication they had a "secret training camp in upstate New York near the back-country town of Argyle," and that they were learning how to shoot machine guns, and carry on guerrilla warfare.

Well, frankly, I didn't believe that. If there was anything like that going on in this County I'd have heard of it. People would have heard of it. Even if it was taking place up by Salem, or down by White Creek.

As a good old friend of mine always used to say: "It doesn't help and it doesn't even matter, but it feels a little better, so why not try?"

Ben Donovan

My best friend in the County. Bendar Bengt are his true first names. I love the guy. Am closer to him even than Jordan Bunch.

We have all known each other since Fort Edward High. Nowadays Ben and I only see each other every other Saturday night during the winter when he and Molly come over to play "pitch" and some other card games.

He works in insurance, but I think if anybody is likely to be honest with you at that racket, he is. He's been with Aetna Life thirty years, I guess. Regional Field Rep.

He and Molly have only one daughter, Bin, in Montreal. No young men in her life yet on a permanent basis.

His hobbies are roller-skating, which he does well all the year around, ice fishing, of which I sometimes enjoy the proceeds, and me.

Drops by every other day at my house during asthma season.

Molly and I, we get along, too, but I can't say we really like each other.

Ben is getting heavy, in the stomach, and these days he has jowls, and soft grey hair, like flax that's been all bleached out, but I remember thinking when I first saw him at age thirteen that only the sun could be so blond, and we have been friends ever since.

It isn't an easy life, for any of us. Ben has a cataract in one eye. All cloudy and pink, and a persistent herpes on his lower lip. He won't use towels when he comes to visit.

His favorite expression is, "Boil me in oil." I love to hear him say that, and "fundamentally," which he divides into two words, as if the second half were about the processes of the head, and the first about anal stuff.

He has been known to drop by to tea at many a local household in the morning to service various of his policies, but Molly, if she knows, always looks the other way.

About every three years Molly is apt to go really "psycho." That spells trouble for my old friend. Last time they found her, after three days, in a phone booth on the outskirts of Vergennes, Vermont. She was cowering and crying and calling Ben "that son of a bitch."

Seems she'd gotten drunk, smashed up her car, and kept on driving north toward Bin till she ran out of gas.

Then she called home and I sent up two of the local kids to get her, and kept Ben company till they returned.

He kept saying, "I don't know what to say."

"What's to say?" I shrugged.

"She has her reasons," Ben said. "It isn't as if she's all to blame, and I'm not."

"I know that," I said, but I poured us more coffee, "and I don't really want to hear about it."

He said, "I don't know how to tell you this . . ."

"Then don't . . ."

"She has just never felt like a woman with me," Ben said, his face all sweaty and yellow.

I said, "None of us can blame each other for that, Ben. Some people are like that. There *are* other things . . ."

"Like what?" He looked at me real fierce, and shook his lank patch of hair back the other way across his forehead.

We were silent as the driveway lit up maybe ten or fifteen minutes later with car lights, and I heard voices, and door slams.

They were back, and Ben was making a fuss over Molly who came in without a coat, looking rubbed red all over her face and arms, and she accepted his attentions, and various ministrations, as if it was only her due, never even looking at me, and they went home together, and nobody ever said a word about that afterwards.

Since then they've seemed pretty close, in fact, though I know Ben waits for the next time, and the next, in his sleep, in his dreams.

God help the poor son of a bitch. But Molly looks fine these days: happy, and rosy, and fat as red applesauce.

Life isn't easy for any of us when you think you have the blood of another all over your hands.

Well, I guess Molly thought she needed insurance more than pleasure so she took Ben as hers, knowing nothing of how much fun he could be, if given half a chance, but expecting—what?—heaven above in Fort Edward.

Now they're both old and discouraged, and Bin has left the house, and I think they must drink a lot. But not that much around me.

A pity, too, because I remember when Molly was a

knockout, and so easy we all thought we wanted to get in her pants, and just because of that (and what our mothers said about her) very few of us ever really did except for Ben who, it seems, could never really please her.

Molly was a hostess in Longchamps in Chicago during the war and I guess she must have had plenty of experience and adventures because her favorite expression when she got back was "smooth as black chiffon." She still uses it sometimes. But when she came back home after her old pa died to stay with Mrs. Anderson awhile, her ma, she never really left again, and the following July the 4th she and Ben met at a picnic, and I knew my old schoolmate had gone and done it. Hooked himself. . . .

Ben's younger brother, Charles, or Chas, as we called him, married a Greek woman and lives in Charleston, South Carolina (he was stationed there during the war), and I'm told he now has seven kids, and a wholesale greengrocer business.

Down there he's practically high society.

Drinks a lot, too.

I used to like the whole family, the names they had for each other: Chas, and Ben was called Bim at home, and he called his ma and pa, as they were real close, Mimou and Pipou. When we were real little Ben was told to call the words for number one and two *sis* and *eh*, or *lunk*, and I was called by the whole family Spinky.

We were all real close. My own ma was sometimes jealous the way I would hang around there, and she didn't like all those pet names we used. Couldn't follow none of that: Mimou Pipou hunky dunky drove her damn near crazy. She wanted to wash my mouth with soap.

Whenever something good happened at home the Donovans would sing and put up signs around the place, and bake cakes. They allowed their children to take a drink at parties, and Mrs. Donovan could play a concertina, and Ben the cornet in German silver.

They sent Chas to Juilliard on a scholarship. He could have been a concert pianist, but he took the easy way out. Marrying money.

As for Mrs. Chas, I only met her one Thanksgiving the year after the war ended. She was pretty and blonde. Her name was Natalie. She knew a lot about old houses.

Maybe I'm wrong, but I think she was flirting with me.

When I asked if she was really a Greek—being so fair—she said her dad was but her "momma was from an old Southern family that's been around as long as you Yankee Spykers, I suppose," and then Charley he apologized for her, but he didn't need to.

Ben wanted us all to gather around the piano, like the old days, but marshmallow-covered sweet potatoes always give me trouble breathing. I figured those two were a doozy together. Told Ben, "It's your party, buster, they're your relations, not mine," and as I excused myself early to walk off the turkey I heard Chas apologizing for my rudeness and good old Ben explaining that I was just getting over things, is all, meaning the Army. . . .

Ben never talks about his brother anymore except when Molly tells about all the servants, and horses, and fancy schools, the trips abroad. Then Ben insists: "Chas really hasn't changed that much. He still likes a good plate of Hoppin' John at the Yacht Club on New Year's Eve," he told me, when Chas had to get a pacemaker for his heart, and I think he's the only member of the family who is sorry Chas chose not to concertize because he was selling insurance by then, and he would have provided, as he says, "come hell or high water."

Whereupon Molly always says, "Get off it, Ben. He's better off and so are we. He never was any Horowitz."

Molly is what you call "a conversation stopper."

Pick a generous impulse and she can make you feel bad about it, and if Ben were still alive I wouldn't be writing any of this, but he's been in a coma the last three months, and I don't think they give him a chance, and I miss him a lot, as I do very few people, my own flesh and blood included.

Phoebe Ainslinger

* *
*

Phoebe Ainslinger was the second of five daughters born to the Ainslinger household in Granville who became so wealthy through their various endeavors that they are, to this day, synonymous with enterprise on the lips of some in the County.

They moved, with their wealth established, to the Falls, and there was born the last three daughters: Jenny, Romolla, and Fay; the eldest being Echo; and there were not yet sons.

To be "wealthy as an Ainslinger heir" soon became figurative of the esteem in which they were held by members of the community. Also to be as "hard-pressed as an Ainslinger servant" was also used, for all the girls, save Phoebe, were stout; and their table was said to be always ample, if not over-abundant.

Ainslingers prospered from quarrying red and black and grey slates from the hills around Granville and Pawlett, Vermont, and their product, even to this day, roofs all the better homesteads in the County. At the height of their prosperity slate floors, and fireplaces, were also luxuries they supplied, and better than five hundred local men were employed, many of them coming from the far-off "calf" of Italy to labor cutting stone. To this day the slate is highly prized and still cut, but under other auspices.

Ainslinger is, of course, a German name of Hanseatic origins, but our clan, latecomers to the County in 1892, were only part-Aryan, the mother being a Syrian woman, dark and squinty-eyed, fierce, though brittle, almost like the slate itself. She was a shrewd businesswoman, too, who called herself, even before her children gave her offspring, Grandma Ainslinger.

She it was who guided the enterprise, for the old man Ainslinger was a philandering drunk, despondent for his old country ways. But when Phoebe came of age she took over.

Grandma Ainslinger, or *Tsadi*, as her brood referred to her affectionately, chose Granville when they came here from abroad, it seems, because of its proximity to mountains and large bodies of water (a flooded inland quarry) after ancient desert nomad custom. She had been daughter of an Arab storekeep in Bremen, where she never felt at home being so dark, when she was proposed to by the old man, Gustave Emmanuel; and they arrived here, like kikes, with pedlar's packs and two small kiddies, and they hoarded up their money and soon were buying up the land and houses.

Ah, they were a dark squinty clan, those five girls, and the boy who died at Dartmouth College (Drusan), all except Phoebe, the beauty, who was dark and slim and shapely, with a rich profusion of lustrous dark long wavy hair that "drove some men wild," lovely soft dark doe eyes as deep as wells, and skin like cocoa butter, but, as luck would have it, she it was who devoted herself, almost entirely, to the business.

Not that she was not much admired by all our young swains, despite her Semite origins, for her animal grace, good looks, quick wits, intelligence, and charm; but I know of only one who can honestly swear he savored of her elixir effluent, and knew in any intimate way that charm, and he prefers to keep *their* secret to his grave.

Phoebe graduated first in her class. If she did not go on to any higher school, it was because she said she was needed to run the family grocery and marry off all her less-well-favored sisters and provide them with dowries. Then she and the baby brother John convinced old *Tsadi* to invest in the quarries.

They prospered so very much more that they began to accumulate a large amount of wealth in cattle and kind, too, and other quarries elsewhere, and they mechanized the work, and paid good wages to the men, while not allowing unions, and they were much admired, as I say, and even envied spitefully, by some, for being foreigners, parasites, "greenies."

Withal they lived modestly; the rumors of barrels of gold in their cellars were simply not true. Though Phoebe, now a grown woman, was admitted to the best of homes, and had many compliments, and flatterers galore, still she did not wed, or openly keep company.

Some said she was no woman at all, but as they call that which holds the water back from flooding over the Hollander's lands.

This I know not to be the case. Her greater passion was her business which she pursued with skill and honesty, and aside from trips to New York every autumn, and Boston every spring, the joys she took were with her young nieces and nephews, who all loved her.

She was the "good aunt," this patient kindly woman. As her beauties faded, she became somewhat peaky-looking, and stern, like aged wood, though never severe.

But Phoebe Ainslinger had this admirer, we now know. Every year on the anniversary of her birth he would send to her a dozen long-stemmed white roses, with a card he never signed except with love, on which were poems such as

> "Despite our worst fears
> we are really one flesh:
> torn from itself;
> tearing itself . . ."

Or,

> "God save us
> From the disaster
> of the aster
> as it withers . . ."

They were all found in a bureau drawer after her going; the tragedy such penned lines veiled.

Some say she died a virgin. Not so. Though her body—even to the end—was that of a ripe young girl, she had known the churl's touch under moonlight when hips sway together and the flesh is one. As it sadly happened, her physical death was sudden and of suspicious causes: at the Cambridge Hospital "of a herpes that signaled hepatitis."

Upon her demise brother John sold the quarries, and moved with his family, including the withered old *Tsadi*, to the Florida Keys where the entire clan of surviving sisters were reunited.

We all mourned that loss, she of the ackee-soft eyes and melon hips had passed among us for so long we had taken her, some of us, for a sister, and to one other, as I say, she was even more: the Heavens themselves, Sun, Moon & Stars, but she was gone now to her Eternal Rest, and the melancholy of her one great passion went right along with her.

But a memorial in the form of a scholarship was established by the clan for young women of the County anxious "to pursue careers in business."

Called "The Phoebe Ainslinger Memorial Fund," this somewhat recondite source entitles any such young woman to a year at the Wharton School of Business in Philadelphia, a second year in Beirut (Lebanon) at the American University, and a lifetime subscription to the *Journal of Mines*, provided that she remain "unfettered by marital ties."

Note the wording: the bequest does not demand virginity, or the unmarried state, but the "unfettered" condition for mercantile life.

It also carries with it this citation: "Family love is a bond thicker than paper, or any debentures of blood, or water. . . .

"Though Phoebe Ainslinger devoted herself to her clan, she pursued a career in business, her slate roofs still sheltering many of us from the inclemencies of weather and alike; and when the final slate was wiped clean she left behind no other posterity save much good will, credit, and cash; hopeful, as she was, that other young women, like herself family-minded, might find a way to enjoy stimulating careers in the exciting and perennial field of mineral extraction without becoming 'in the family way.'

"To perpetuate her memory, then, and honor her success, this two-year stipend has been awarded to (name of grantee, or designee)."

Now some would say that the preponderance of independent and strong-willed women in the County among men of weak wills and flatulent moral vigor says something about the human condition north of Albany. Sad to say, Phoebe Ainslinger's favorite niece, Roberta Ellen (whom they called Barbi) was the first and, until recently, the only recipient of such aid, and she ran off with an instructor in a health club in New York, and lives now in Greenwich Village—a life of shabby bohemian elegance—and may God spare this lovely young treasure from her aunt's lonely end.

Everett Clincher

* *
 *

Everett Clincher was a Hollobird. The Hollobirds married Pelters and Smudgeons. Everett's ma, Jeannette, was the sister of Mavis Pelter.

He wasn't much by himself except for a set of queer beliefs he set down in his journals and left in a Safe Deposit Box at the First Trust & Deposit, a Pelter enterprise.

Everett believed he was spiritually the descendant of Egyptian and Babylonian kings.

Proof was his rather dark complexion and memories of a hot sunny land.

He was no mere reincarnationist, for Everett also believed: "As I have been passed through eternity from generation to generation, and nation to nation has known of me, so I bequeath no other legacy save my corpse to my heirs, that they must endeavor, in every way, to preserve me against the Resurrection. If, in fifty years, my body remains intact, and not too ripe, they shall be rewarded with my estate."

Thus Everett's fame rests largely on something that happened after his death: his only son Aaron, and his wife Sharon, tried to arrange to have him mummified.

But the art was lost on our local undertakers; and, while Everett remained on ice, inquiries were made as far away as New York, New York, and Boston, without any positive answers ensuing.

The local taxidermist, Miller Wilson, was called in. He had worked on nothing larger than the head of a deer, but said he would be certainly willing to try, for a good fee, if he could be indemnified against possible prosecution by the law for an illegal pursuit.

Again inquiries were made, and the answer was no: A man could not be preserved as one preserved a large-mouthed bass, or a bear's paw. It went against all the health codes.

There was in Saratoga a certain Professor Morgenstern who practiced "galvanic preservation," he claimed, with marvelous results. By introducing electrodes into the anus and the mouth of the deceased and passing through the cadaver a sustained and powerful charge, the flesh would be made to tan, almost like leather, and the linings of the body would be "electrolytically" sealed.

Everett had been on ice two weeks. The expense was staggering; the odor had to be avoided. The heirs agreed for a fee of $750 to try out this new method of embalming.

The corpse was transported to Saratoga in an ice truck. All was made ready for the electrical wonder, but kept hush-hush to avoid a crowd forming.

Professor Morgenstern applied the electrodes and turned on the juice; Everett fried to a deep brownish yellow almost like goose grackle.

The Professor was out his fee; the heirs lost their estate; and Everett's corpse went to the cemetery and his holdings were sold at auction and turned over to the Comptroller, the State of New York, after a legal fight that lasted many years.

All this goes to prove, I suppose, that life here and

now is infinitely more desirable than to await the resurrection, as man, or fly, or fowl, in another life.

But Everett's life was a source of wonderment on more than just this account. When attorneys for the State were going through the journals and account books, they found many queer and wonderful sentiments expounded.

Everett believed God was the reincarnation of the Devil, our true First Cause, and Prime Mover.

He wrote, "As I am God's servant, so was I the Devil's helper."

He called himself, "Natchywanger," and nobody knew why, or what that meant.

He said he had never been "so sinful as when I was virtuous."

He accused God of abandoning his late wife to "putrefaction," declared himself a Democrat in politics, and a celibate until Eternity, and warned all his fellow townspeople against sleeping with their mates.

As he saw it, the problem was one of "animal magnetism" being exchanged through such a commerce so that the man became womanish and she masculinized: "There is nothing that will derange the nervous system quite like a person who is eliminative in nature lying abed all night with a person who is nervous in nature," wrote Everett. "For the one will wake up perkish and the other sluggish. . . ."

Everett believed these traits were passed on down the generative ladder of history through reincarnation so that "eliminative" persons ended up as slugs and snails and "nervous" persons were apt to be crickets and darning needles.

Not a bit of sense in any of this, of course, but I have gone into it at some length so that we may all better understand how some weave nets of lies to catch their lives in before they surrender to that final lassitude.

Everett Clincher is buried in the Pelter family plot, along with Hollobirds, Clinchers, and Smudgeons.

His words are a grander monument than his headstone, which is small, tablet-like, of white marble, inscribed only with:

"He tried
But fried."

Budgy Bordelaise

*** *
*

One thing I never liked was a man who lied a lot, and that applies to a woman, too, which is why I never had much use for Budgy Bordelaise.

They used to call her "Make A Wish Come True" and "Miss Falseface." I wonder why.

She told me she had been on Mars once.

She told other people how she was a full-blooded gypsy when we all knew she was just Frenchy scum from up north.

When she used to go to Troy she said she'd been to New York.

She lied so much you couldn't get the weather straight from her, or the time of day.

She told Mayor Wasser she could leave her own body and fly.

She told Erny Ames she knew how to make Indian pudding, and then she served MY-T-Fine.

Nothing was too small to lie about.

Budgy told my old ma once she could split into a man and a woman and then make love to herself.

Some people believed her, but I never did: How she knew the language of sheep and pigs. Making all those horrible grunts, and squeals; and how she claimed to like eating dirt.

Some people said she was just "very sick in the

head" ("You know," they'd add, with a wink, as their big fingers circled their temples). But I say she just lied a lot and that was just her way is all because she didn't much care for other people and what they thought of her, or what she got from them.

I don't know how she ever got on. Eventually she took work in the Howland mansion as a sort of cook's helper, but her habits were too filthy, and she would never stop lying. Cook would ask, "Did you pepper the stew?" She would say yes, and it would turn out not to be true.

Then they set her to work telling stories to kiddies at the Public Library after school and that worked out, for a while, though the money wasn't very much. She was just like a kid, too, in some ways, only a bigger liar.

She died eventually, having been born in 1859, as it turned out; and that was during the war with Korea, and she was very very old, almost a hundred. Erny Ames bought her a cheap funeral and paid for the headstone. It says : "This is no lie, Budgy."

Lauterbach The Physician
* *
*

A foremost surgeon, known throughout the Counties and the Upper Hudson Valley, Ernst Lauterbach used to boast he could "cut" without drawing blood.

He raised horses, and fighting cocks, had a yellow rooster named Dan Patch.

He married with a female agronomist, Pru Gaines.

They had no offspring.

He grew very wealthy on appendectomies, and caesarean sections.

They say he left over a million dollars in a wall safe in cash upon his going, but Pru knew the combination and found it and took most of what there was to do research on the melon.

Later, she went off with Lopat Hymes, a local poetaster and dilettante, to the Continent where they were never heard from again.

When Lauterbach passed on, a local editorialist noted: "His scalpel was everyman's ally. He was privy to the secrets of the belly and the gut. He was as much a part of this community as if he had been fastened to us, with a silken suture."

Lauterbach perfected an operation for the relief of hemorrhoids.

His large mansion in Queensbury was also his

159

office. The shingle was fastened to a wrought-iron lamppost on the lawn:

> *"Dr. Ernest Lauterbach*
> *By Appointment.*
> *Entrance In the Rear."*

Lou Lanergan

* *
 *

The singularly most attractive aspect of Lou Lanergan was he had been a great war hero.

In the Japanese campaigns he shot down twenty enemy Zeros.

Had his photographs taken for *Life* magazine and came home to a parade.

He was a modest man and said it was "all just blind luck."

"I felt like I was lucky," Lou said, "and that's all there is to it. I was pretty scared most of the time."

The father, Emmett, had political dreams and he mortgaged the family hardware store to send Lou on to law school at McGill and then when he came back he convinced his son, the hero, to run for County Prosecutor.

Lou's campaign posters said, "He shot down 20 Zeros and now he will fight crime, too, in Washington County."

He won by a big enough margin, as he was a Republican.

All went well enough, I suppose, except Lou was restless. He preferred duck hunting. He had no taste for politics.

In those days nobody had ever been tried for murder in the County for fifteen years, and Lou aimed to keep it that way. But he was hard on crooks. He prosecuted a phony dairying cooperative which happened to be operated by the brother of the GOP chairman, as a blind, and when asked to lay off, persisted.

He got convictions, too, which was rare for the County in those days, but he did not get the nomination to be Prosecutor another time.

He may have been a great war hero once, but now he was just another jerkwater lawyer.

The father stopped speaking to him, too.

People said he was "an individualist" and "a solitary drinker until the day he died."

Naomi Flegg & Triplicatism

*** *
*

That there is a garden below death; that we are apt to stumble among its flagrant growths and weedy precincts in our journey through life; and that men should be orderly in all their ways, like peas in a pod, were only some of the more available precepts of Triplicatism, an odd ethical doctrine promulgated by Naomi Flegg of Argyle.

She was a teetotaler and, to this day, the town remains dry.

She was a greengrocer's wife and much of the imagery of her queer faith derives from fruits and vegetables.

Naomi believed all human life swarmed about itself "like the volutes on a large cauliflower," but that order and peace came from "an unwrinkling of intricacies, ultimate symmetries."

Triplicatism, which she founded, was a Church without an edifice. They would meet together in the fields to pray.

The faith believed in the magic of threes: there had been three historical Christs, for example, though Naomi only knew of two. In 1896 she walked all the way to Fort Ti, trekking by night, and sleeping by day, to follow a star she believed would announce the birth of the third Christ; and, when she found nothing so much like that, she announced to her few followers that Christ was a fisher of men's souls "and of the bullhead pike in Lake Champlain near Fort Henry."

She was regularly denounced by the leaders of the Roman and Episcopate churches for offenses of such great magnitude against theological doctrine I know not how to recount them in such small space here. Naomi and her followers believed the Godhead was as flagrant as the dandelion weed. She wrote in *The Triplicate Christ:* "Just as our Lord suffered and died so men might know salvation, consider the humble dandelion that every year rises from the earth and spreads its golden crown before it succumbs to the diurnal round and is detritus."

The Triplicate Christ was a slim pamphlet of less than one hundred pages which sold fifty times that number of copies every year for a decade among the residents of Washington County, and some people then called her the Mormon Woman because, though she was not a Latter-day Saint, she seemed to have some commonality to that other great nineteenth century heresy from our part of the State.

At last Naomi and her husband and a few of their followers decided Canada was a more likely place for a Third Coming, and they bought land in the district of Ontario around Petawawa where, as far as I know, they still practice their odd doctrines, including triplicate circumcision, and continue to pray in the fields.

Wavey Blakey

* *
*

Her Christian name was Eleanor. She was part Italian, and a Papist. A substantial woman of good looks, and womanly figure. A physical person. She had been a dairywoman not too far out of town, on her parents' home, on the flats, heading toward Argyle, and then she married Blakey and moved to town, since he ran the snowplow for the township, and they made two fine boys together, strapping fellows, and they seemed happy.

Blakey took a strange malady of the blood complicated by an ileitis, such as Eisenhower had, and after a year he died. She buried him and came home to an empty house, since the boys were now in school at Fredonia and Oswego, and she was lonely, pretty, and lusty, a woman like that, and after about a year she began to look peaky, and some people said she was drinking a lot by herself.

She was left some insurance, and she did not have to work, so she began to sew fancy things for herself, and others, on special order, and she had this little shop in her home. Still, she did not seem happy.

Then she must have bumped into Mellerstein, the German mechanic from the VW showroom, and he moved in with her, and she seemed a little happier. Hearty again.

They tried to have a child together, as she was still of child-bearing age, but she produced a mongoloid, Florence, named, I suppose, after her mother's birthplace, and that thing lived only three years with them before dying.

Yet they remained happy together.

Wavey told the Boggs woman that Mellerstein "took no interest in anything but his cars and yours truly," and that "he really knew the difference."

I believe if their child had been born normal they would have surely married.

Still, they stayed together.

She had a lovely warm soprano voice and could sing "Santa Lucia" and other period songs, including one in Russian she called "Stenka Rossen."

People called her Wavey from when she was a child. Her hair was black and flowing over rapids of waves and kinks: as she got older it straightened on her and she wore it in a large French bun.

"Born Again" Bengston

* *
 *

Born the first time Boyd T. Bengston he became a Christian late in his forties, as if this was some sort of moral climacteric he was going through; and so the neighbors dubbed him "Born Again" Bengston to indicate the second birth of God in his Soul which he proclaimed to one and all, loudly, and often.

His second birth coincided with his becoming considerably well-off from the sale of a sister's farmstead near Little Tupper to a group of speculators from New York, New York, who were putting up a ski resort; and there was some local speculation, too, that the sister, a widow, had not died in her sleep of natural causes, but nobody ever pointed his finger at "Born Again" and made it stick; people just said wasn't he lucky to get God and money all at once; and that's sort of what "Born Again" said, too, whenever he testified.

He'd been in the cesspool line, but never made a real go of it, and so to speak had his hands full with his creditors and incompetent workers and what not, and then he came into fifty thousand dollars which, in 1946, was still a lot of money. So "Born Again" sold the business, or rather what he had in bills outstanding, to a collection company that was a sideline for one of the Harlands; and then he bought up a whole block of wooden flats in Mechanicville opposite to one of the mills and went to live in Florida in a small town outside Jacksonville.

He grew mutton-chop sideburns and a deep tan and he wore Hawaiian shirts whenever he came north to see to the upkeep of his properties in late spring, and he got him a young dyed-blonde born-again wife, and they born themselves a little boy whom they called Billy Sid, after both their fathers, I guess; and then we only heard about him, as he became exceedingly rich, when the flats were destroyed for urban renewal, and he didn't come north any longer except he would send press releases to all the local papers about his various activities: how he'd preached salvation to a conference on Hilton Head Island, and attended a prayer breakfast at the White House; about his son graduating from the Naval Academy; and the wife, Sue Ellen, birthing them both a young daughter at, we figured, at least age forty-two.

I believe the people of the County were pretty impressed with what it meant to be born again in the case of Bengston, but there were some who pointed out it hadn't been so good the first time he was put on earth so he had every right to expect a little better the second time he conceived Eternity inside himself, and nobody was that envious. It's been a long time since we had the sort of folks as would spend the first forty years of their life taking care of other people's shit for a crack at the Hereafter.

Armand The Urning

* *
 *

A rather peculiar version of the so-called Man–Woman lived in Sandy Hill for many years and we called him Armand The Urning.

That title comes about because, though Armand looked like any other man I know, approximately (having two arms and legs and a fullish chest, rather short-cropped hair), he was so very very pale, his breasts, perhaps, a little better formed than most, and he had these pouting fullish lips. Also, a smooth-ish face and long blond eyelashes.

Inside his manly body he was an Urning; there was a woman blushing. Armand cried easily; he was just full of fluids and sweetness, as sensitive as a louse-bite.

He made a living nursing the sick; he was very accomplished at relieving suffering, and also excellent in caring for small children, and invalids. People said he had the softest hands, a delicate touch.

He did nothing indelicate; he was never lewd or provocative. Maybe a trifle prissy.

I used to see him very often as he walked to his various cases in a white smock and trousers; he had a distinctive waddle, a sort of a splay-footed walk. He was very large from behind, almost albinoish fair.

He was always friendly, always stopped to chat

about the weather. Cold days made him look sad. But we were never attracted to each other.

This Urning male had an Urning female friend, Gloxy, who also lived in Fort Edward. She was heavy, with a basso voice, a mustache. She wore ribbons in her hair, dressed the female.

I do not know if they were ever lovers, but all the small boys said so after spying on them, and they were called by the townsfolk Vice-Versa whenever they were seen together. The small boys would chase them down streets and curse at them.

When Gloxy died Armand grew meager and sad. Then he took a boy into his household, a mere lad, hardly more than a child, and there were the usual rumors, of course, but nobody really knew.

You would just see them walking down the street together, hand in hand, with the tears running off their faces.

Armand trained the lad as his assistant, and he became a passable fair nurse, and midwife.

His name was Ginger because he had this purplish-red hair that later turned a sort of maroon.

Well, so then the boy left him, too, on growing up, for one of the larger cities, San Francisco, as I recall, and Armand The Urning, having seen a lot of dying, was alone with himself again.

He just looked very very sad, as pale as cocoanut milk. Wane.

When my own ma was ailing that final time I had him come in and help out. He was a great comfort to Ma, I think, in those final days. Made soups for her, and rubbed her back with mint leaves and alcohol, brewed herb tea. Read to her. Mostly, just through the talking.

I guess it was then he first told me about the colony

of Urning men and women down by the Mettawee in Whitehall, though he called them, simply, "oddities and crudities."

I later visited the place with my artistical friend, Crow Marie, the painter, and I must say that was quite an experience. They had this large old green farmhouse and barn, but they neither farmed, nor raised herds. Mostly they wove things, like tea cosies and mats, and there was a potter, too, who made vases with large ears.

I bought one from the fellow for a lady friend and when I gave him the money he cried, just like Armand, big salty tears.

There was also a maker of Indian moccasins, and a fellow who confected natural cosmetics, soaps, and notions. He had made himself a gold-lettered sign: "The Shampoo of Bottled Beers."

Crow Marie said they were fairies, but I don't know; they all had women with them.

Well, I guess it takes all kinds. You know, these Urnings are very sensitive to the least little slights, remarks good or bad. They say there was one down in White Creek even used to menstruate every other month.

When Armand was seventy Sandy Hill gave him a little testimonial in the Veterans' Memorial Park, and a scroll with hand letters was presented for all his kindnesses to people at their last hours, and then he sang, in a piping little falsetto, "None But the Lonely Heart" and "I Walked Through the Garden Alone."

He had a truly lovely sweet expression on his Urning face when he sang, as if he were being kissed, and pretty soon everybody was crying along with him, except for Fathead Kelly who called us all "a bunch of damn sissies."

The last I saw of him was when he had a yard sale because he planned to spend his declining years as a masseur in one of the resorts of the British Islands of the Caribbean.

He sold out everything: ormolu clocks, and frilly dresses, two brass beds, a velveteen love seat.

I bought his old toaster for a cousin on relief, and his book on first aid.

When we shook hands goodbye I could swear he tickled my palm. A friendly tickle. . . .

Others may tell you he was maybe part, or whole, blow fish because he always had this fishy smell about him (from taking cod-liver oil), but I can tell you he had an extremely wet palm which is suspicious to some.

So then he was gone and all we had to remember Armand by was the many tender things he did for people when they were ailing, like the back rubs, making beds, going to the store; so then some people said he was just a great big Nancy and a queer, to boot, and let it go at that. Well, I don't know. Armand was awful strong. I once saw him lift Spence Coleman's bull by the back legs to keep it from trampling Sissy Roebuck's right arm, and he knew a lot of strange things, too, like Indian lore. He built a Sioux teepee out of birch logs and skins, piled dead leaves and new snow around the base, and lived in it all of one winter with that boy Ginger, and when you asked him what it was like inside Armand always said, "Cozy as pie."

That was his favorite expression: "Cozy as pie."

Bonar Thomas

He was a Welshman. He raised sheep. He lived alone.
The schoolboys called him Boner.

    I know very little else about the man except he had
a brother with an unpronounceable name near Amsterdam, and he was trampled by an ox once in the
Romaree Corral.

Kissy Kigeloff

* *
 *

The sister of the owner of the Boston Store, a dry goods emporium. She was dark and pretty. She had lots of beaus but never married. They say she was a lezzy. I don't know, but maybe she was just shy. They called her Kissy because she was so shy. At graduation she went to get her diploma and lost her Vel Down right in the middle of the stage.

Bart Kigeloff

Proprietor of the Boston Store. He came and went a lot to Boston and New York. He wore braces and spats. He used to suck peppermint breath-lozenges, and called everybody "Pal."

His favorite expression was, "Takes one to know one."

Died in Florida, I believe, along with sister Kissy.

Naomi Kigeloff

Bart's wife. Totally and thoroughly undistinguished
except they say she drove every Friday morning to
Troy to buy Kosher meat for the week.

Vartas Vartun

* *
  *

A Persian carpet merchant by that name moved to the Falls from Chicopee Falls, and promptly failed at business. Since he was a Bahai he had no few cohorts. He opened a small restaurant and, like a Greek, would serve none of his own national dishes, but hamburgers, and fried potatoes, griddle cakes, rice pudding, and fried dough.

He failed again at that. We wondered who was staking him. He took no outside jobs and lived very meagerly.

Vartas called both his carpet shop and the restaurant The Eastern Star. Now, as if to change his luck, he embarked on quite another business venture: The Scimitar Laundry.

Some people didn't know what the word meant, or how to spell it, and my old friend Ben remarked how many scimitars could there be in Washington County that needed laundering.

That business failed, too.

Vartas was doing something wrong. He was a dark glowering man, looked a lot like a Red Indian with colic.

Vartas had never known the joy of life.

He missed the sunshine and roses.

He also seemed quite misinformed about the local business climate.

In truth, he was so miserable without his family that it was almost like they're being here.

When his laundry failed Vartas sent for his three oldest daughters from Persia and started a pizzeria. On the side the girls also read palms, and tea leaves.

He prospered and set one girl up in her own separate submarine shop, and then imported another, the belle of the lot, and she he made an airline stewardess so that she might get well-married.

He then opened another small store he called a hobby shop in which he sold tropical fish and electrical trains, and balsa wood models. This, too, like all his other enterprises, he called the Persian Hobby Shop.

There was the Persian Pizzeria.

The Persian Submarine Shop.

The Persian Hobby Shop.

My friend Ben joked the only Persian hobby he ever knew of was whipping the dummy.

Vartas prospered. He became an Elk, a Lion, Chamber of Commerce, and all the rest.

When interviewed some years later about the secret of his fabulous business acumen in the *Post Star* he explained, "This is America and you should never be ashamed of who you are here because we are all immigrants here, even Columbus."

Vartas' favorite expression was, "Give me back my boots and saddles."

The *Post Star* interview depicted him as "looking a lot like comedian Danny Thomas." When I asked Vartas how he felt about that he said he was flattered, of course, what else, and so on and so forth.

Then he bought into an automatic car wash on the

Boulevard, and first he called it the Persian Car Wash, but when it went broke he reorganized as Danny Thomas' Automat.

Did very well at that, too, and bought a big estate outside [Lake] Luzerne he called Persian Acres.

He met a beautiful Parsee woman from Bombay, India, at the Merchandise Mart in Chicago while on a buying trip and married her and brought her to his home. This is a story with sort of a happy ending: Vartas and she were able to produce a son, Nizzim Hikmet, and when he got old he spent about six months out of every year in Pernambuco, Brazil, where he had a brother, and in Maracaibo, where his mother's uncle lived.

A truly freak accident involving one of the hoses at the car wash was his undoing. He was "steamed to death" like a lobster.

Mr. Bon Giorno

*   *
  *

An Italian laborer and his family moved to Sandy Hill,
our first, about 1910. His name was Benevenuti, or
Benevenuto, I can't remember which, but everybody
used to call him Mr. Bon Giorno because that's what
he used to say when he met you on the street.

He took a job with Sandy Hill Company in the
castings division as an oiler. Immediately he had
his arm crushed by one of the giant presses. Then he
couldn't work any more. The wife, who was healthy
and fat, became the breadwinner for the whole family.
She opened a cafe not far from the factory where the
men would go for a good cheap lunch and a beer. The
man became her greeter, and he drew beer from the
barrels. To everybody he had the same greeting: *"Bon
giorno!"*

A big silly grin on his face whenever he played
dominoes.

All his factory mates liked the Italian and they
patronized his cafe. The family prospered. When the
daughter was of age they married her off to an Italian
from Schenectady and set them up in a pizzeria in
Cambridge, New York.

Mr. Bon Giorno gardened and raised tomatoes and
hot peppers. He brought over his sister from the old

country and bought her a house next door to his own off Ethan Allen, and then they built a small summer house for the daughter and her husband on the same property. They raised tomatoes in such abundance that they began to sell off some of the stuff they had canned and bottled as a sauce under their own label, "Mrs. Bene's," and a lot of local people preferred that to Franco-American, Chef Boyardee, etc.

This is a success story, I think. When the poor overworked wife died Mr. Bon Giorno married again, to a cousin of his sister-in-law, I was told, who lived in Tarpon Springs, Florida. The business was closed and the family moved away, all except the daughter who is still here.

No more sauce in bottles, though: that was strictly the mother's affair. The daughter and her husband are now in real estate.

The old man liked to nip the dago red a lot. He had a lot of pain from that arm and a very red face, almost just like a tomato, a big guinea stinker in his mouth at all times, and in the summer he always wore dark suit pants and an undershirt while gardening.

A nice old man, I think; he had lots of *paisanos* here after a while, and he must have been pretty good with the ladies, too, even with just one arm. He had also two sons, Diamond and Ruffi, and another daughter, Celestina, who we called Cele. She married with an executive at G.E. in Pittsfield, Massachusetts, and last I heard was moving to Marcellus outside Syracuse.

What else? Mr. Benevenuti didn't like Jews. He called them all "money lenders" though we had none of that sort in our community; and during the war everybody made fun of Mussolini to him and he would get very angry and call us all a bunch of "no goods." But the son Diamond was killed at Anzio and then everything was all right with people. The family was considered as American as anybody then, even though they still hardly spoke any English.

Vitas Smith

* *
  *

On the argument that men are sometimes just and fair
with one another and the Divine Providence does not
necessarily play favorites, Vitas Smith contended in
the negative. He was no knee-jerker to liberal senti-
mentality, no moron of good will. Life was just very
cruel, Vitas insisted; there must be suffering, inequal-
ity, and misery to lift some above the common lot of
their fellows.

But his arguments seemed rather academic:
Vitas married money, and lived well. He wintered in
Palm Beach, and summered on a farm outside Greenwich. He never worked, and seemed somehow to have
entirely avoided the struggle for survival he recommended to others. He was a man of becoming round-
ness, and blondness; at thirty a plump satisfied belly
went before him on his daily rounds. He was no
yachtsman, nor equestrian, did not sport in any way,
or collect things, but he had a hobby. Vitas loved
wars.

His library was a collection of full-color illustrated
books on the history of uniforms and carnage. He
went about the world inspecting battlefields. He cor-
responded with the generals and military historians.

"It is the ritual purification of a nation's blood,"
Vitas would say. "The ultimate test of any man's will
to survive."

On his Greenwich farm Vitas had reproduced a replica of the trench systems of the Somme. He volunteered to serve when the Japanese attacked Pearl Harbor and, because of his great wealth and knowledge of history, was assigned to the OSS.

This made Vitas very discontented. To serve without a uniform at the inglorious task of "intelligence" was hardly what his desires and ambitions had been pointing him toward; he thought he would be relegated to a desk job in some dim inglorious corner of the War Department but he was sent abroad, to England, and trained to be a secret agent and spy. Vitas' superiors reasoned, logically enough, that the man was so ludicrous in his afflatus his true mission would not be perceived. It became Vitas' job to hobnob with British military personnel of the highest orders, persons much like himself, and to report back on what he could learn to his Intelligence superiors.

Apparently, he performed quite well, and was decorated, though again not in any way he could display publicly, and after the war he volunteered to stay on with the Intelligence Service, eventually gaining employment on an irregular basis with the CIA. This man, with the charm of a blunderbuss, and the subtlety of a blob of gellagnite, became a leading spook in the service of his country, and throughout the years of peaceful Cold War he deployed himself to commit murder and espionage, encourage treason, and provoke embarrassing incidents. For so ridiculous was the figure he cut in the world, this windbag, this Blimp, with his martial appetites, and his outspoken joy at carnage, that he was believed to be a mere goose. An amateur. Nobody to take seriously.

It's often the case that the most successful cover one can have is to be simply oneself. Vitas Smith was so barbarously out of step with the postwar world that nobody ever considered he might be one of its most instrumental figures until some six months before his scheduled retirement, when on a holiday among the ruined pillboxes along the coast of Normandy, he was noticed by a Soviet defector and double agent who had seen him previously on one of his rare visits to the agency's central headquarters in Langley.

Then Vitas Smith was targeted for a "hit." "Having been a witness to current history," Vitas wrote in his Normandy diaries, "I find I still do not despair in the infinite power of men to inflict grave injuries on one another. The only sure emetic to the emotionalisms of our era is to see what a man looks like after he has been blown limb from limb by a Claymore mine."

It would be nice to add, if one could, that such violence of thought inseminated further violence as retribution, but Smith met a clean, swift, presumably painless end when a cyanide dart was injected into his neck as he ate a supper of pheasant stuffed with oysters in the main dining salon of the Hôtel du Golf at Deauville.

In the local papers his demise was reported as a "heart attack," under the headline: "PROMINENT GREENWICH MAN DIES ABROAD." But Violet Smith, the wife, when she returned from abroad, told the truth of her husband's strange career and his ultimate misfortune to a sister of Betty Harland, and she told me. Then Violet married again, to a defrocked priest from the Carmelite retreat in Lake Placid, and the two moved to Italy where they lead the sweet life, I presume, beside the still waters of Lake Como: he translating Leopardi, and she attempting to write a novel based on the adventures of the man she lived with for better than thirty years and always assumed was just a braggart, a bully, and a fool.

Paris Wasser

* *
   *

People named him after the French capital because he came back from Belgium after the Great War singing that song about "how ya gonna keep 'em down on the farm?"

Nevertheless, he stayed on his farm outside Gansevoort and never again tried to leave home until World War II when he drove up to Canada and volunteered to serve as a mechanic with the RCAF, but was rejected for a hernia.

Then he went back to his golden-haired wife and grown children on the farm and never left there any more for a longer spell than a weekend.

A regular sort of fellow and gay and pretty nice, too, but no war hero. Served as a muler in the Mule Transports Corps handling the mules, and later repaired caissons.

He had a funny way of ploughing his fields in a series of concentric figure eights, and he raised a heck of a lot of Jerusalem artichokes, kept bees, and took a very expensive imported snuff from Finland—his only real luxury, in so far as I know—and was a regular adult advisor to the Future Farmers of America.

His wife was an Arsdale from Smith's Basin. People say they dropped the "Van" during the Great War to avoid anti-German feelings.

Had a brother played pretty good first base for the Pittsfield Electrics.

They give him a tryout with the Red Sox.

Paris was so very tall and rangy, maybe six foot or more, you didn't always notice he weighed better than two hundred pounds naked in the shower.

Once he got into a fight with Arly Davis about proper Christian beliefs.

Arly said a sinner was damned unto his perdition and for all eternity (or words to that effect) and Paris maintained there would always be forgiveness, like summer thunder storms, from the Merciful Christ who is our Savior, even unto the Last Trump.

Well, they finally said they would debate it all one Sunday fair and square after Congregational Church services with Minister Muller to moderate and show them the various ins and outs of all their theological tickles and so forth, but when the great day arrived they promptly forgot about it, fearing to get too personal in front of their respective wives.

The next time they met was opposite to the old opera house in Fort Edward (that place that is now the wholesale butcher) and there was this little kid in front of the Stewart's Ice Cream licking on a strawberry cone and Arly said he looks just like you Paris, as do a heck of a lot of the local kids, and how do you explain all that?

And then he spat at Paris a big brown gobbet.

Paris didn't like being talked about in that way, much less spat at, so he stove Arly into the side of his Ford pickup.

Or maybe it was a Chevvy 2. Can't recall. . . .

The thing was everybody in the County knew of Paris' peccadillos but nobody ever talked out loud in public because he was usually such a gentle sweet guy most people figured Arly must have deserved something or other; and, besides, he never pressed any charges, being on the County at the time.

When he was too old to work his land, Paris did lotsa odd jobs. He kept a big Sears Diehard storage battery in his Chevvy and gave jumps to people during the winter at the Glens Falls Airport (and sometimes in Albany) when they left their cars overnight and couldn't get them started up again.

He charged you $5 but he got you going.

Paris was left wifeless at fifty, which is young for a man or a woman, and some people said he would sometimes do rude things to women in the church vestibule.

When Arly died P was among the pallbearers. His favorite expression was: "Soft as a lady's . . ."

Sam Kardin (aka Sam Spam)

* *
*

He was Chief Dietician and, later, Warder at the Comstock State Prison in Whitehall (only they don't call them that anymore and the prison is called a "correctional facility"); and he became a very rich man, people say, and retired and collected ormolu clocks.

I won't say he stole outright, but he kept all the prisoners on pretty short rations and he and his Mrs. must have gotten pretty used to having lotsa servants near the Big House and it was the State asked him to step down early at half his superannuation and he then purchased this large spread on the Vaughn Road and filled it with ormolu clocks from all over the world, and he also collected various types of rifles and shotguns.

He owned a camp on Lake Luzerne where he ice-fished.

Stood well over five foot ten, I would say, and must have weighed two hundred fifty pounds in his prime: A big raw face like a smoked pork butt.

Had a hound dog for hunting he called Fem because of the way she would sniff at herself and others, and he always wore white buck shoes, summer or winter, or maybe white and black saddle shoes.

People said of him he was so tight he could stretch jello.

Dead.

Goldy Fahrenholtz

*　*
　*

Called Golly by some, and Girly. Hair like a summer wheatfield and a bosom so big and round it kept most men strangers to her, except in a business way; but she was regular and bonnyroo, alright, and could give you a loving that would keep your knees buckling a whole month, or more.

Ran a "blind pig" behind the G.E. for thirty years and during the real hard times she even accepted food stamps, and stuff like crops for barter.

Some men called her "the Greek lady"; but when she died they held her wake in Polish and twenty of our best young studs from the VFW volunteered to be her pallbearers.

Her favorite expression was: "I eat what I like and I like what I eat."

Once, some wiseacre quipped: "Why not eat me, Goldy?"

"Ah," she said. "Golly, I just couldn't right now."

"Well, why in hell not?"

"I've taken the penance for Easter, for Lent," she explained. "I'm fasting."

The fellow persisted: "What about the other way?"

"No harm in that," Goldy said, with a grimace. "None whatsoever. I'll just regard that as a form of garbage disposal."

I really miss old Goldy because she knew how to get your goat but once she got it she always give it a little petting with her hand and maybe something for a treat, like her old tin cans.

Bonita Fetlock

Third daughter of the Fetlocks of Butternut Grove,
she finally found herself as a person in her own right
on the eve of Franklin Roosevelt's second election
when she baked more than ten thousand toll-house
cookies in his image, complete with a cigarette holder,
and passed them out from door to door.

That was perhaps the first time a Democrat got a
large vote in the County, and people still say it was
Bunny Fetlock's doing.

I always thought she was the most beautiful of all
the Fetlock girls, the most breathtaking in our class at
school, and I am sorry if her life was sad for I loved her
dearly, and would have married with her, if she was to
be had, and to this day have a crush and must look
away whenever we pass hobbling across the corner of
Main and Maple, but she is with a Bascomber, and has
been thirty years or more, and they say he drinks, and
she takes sleeping pills.

Such a pity. Such a spirited thing. Their only son
died in Vietnam and was sent home headless in a
sealed casket.

Boog Hollander

* *
  *

His real name was Beverly, and his wife's name was
Barbi. They raised swine, the most economical of
beasts, and prospered. He was expert at the sticking,
and made a fine blood sausage. Also chitterlings, and
smoked butts, in a chiphouse he had erected behind
the pig pens.

People called him Mr. Pig Himself, and kept their
distance.

He came in a truck once a week for our potato
peelings, and we thought that was for his pigs, too,
but later learned he ran a still.

He was almost always drunk, and the wife went to
town shopping and, they say, sometimes forgot her
step-ins.

This most odious couple prospered so that they
acquired land in Florida, and built condominiums
upon retiring, and collected rents.

Some people said that was basically the same as
when they had kept pigs.

His favorite expression was, "Let me jolly your
buns awhile."

She always would say, "Do yourself a favor and
take a look at my twat."

They had no children, but kept swineherd boys as

apprentices, except they eventually all ran off elsewhere.

The people of Dutchtown Road said that the big mountains behind Argyle were called Green because they had smelled Hollander's farm.

Gauntly Spinker

* *
 *

Our cousin, commonly called Gaunt, skinny as a Red Indian, and orphaned at or near birth.

He lived with us once briefly before going off with Pershing to chase Pancho Villa.

He had a trust fund, and his only friend lived in Greenwich and collected ladies' and gents' hats of all ages.

Gaunt had no hobbies, and no recreations that we all knew of, except it was rumored widely he could masturbate with either hand, a feat that elicited almost as much admiration as it did shock, dismay, and so forth.

He was a poor soldier, it seems, and was sent home for "moral cowardice" by Pershing, a crime that was, apparently, a euphemism for the self-abuse.

When he came back he joined the National Guards and drove the little tank on parades, and became an air-raid warden during World War II, and for a while ran a shop in Salem where he sold used carburetors, and other such devices, and then went broke, and my records show filed for bankruptcy and married the daughter of Dyke, the railroad paymaster, and they say he could not interest himself in husbandliness for long, and soon was at himself again, night and day, until he had yanked what little substance there was in him across all his carpets and bedsheets, and he became dank, and sallow, and was cuckolded, and separated from her, divorced, and remarried, to a widow from Queensbury, Mrs. Onderder.

So much for the life as such. He had no peculiar traits aside from what I have mentioned, which in those unenlightened days was regarded as merely odious, and when he sat in the motion-picture show people said he ate his own bogers.

Well, so do many, I suppose. I never shunned him, nor was he not welcome at my house. Nor was he ever invited to sup with me after Mamma died.

I thought, he succors himself well enough, and I must also think of our costly upholstered chairs.

He left me a small annuity on dying, and his will declared that I was his favorite kin. He wrote, "To be Spinker when you know you are Spyker is that cruel disability from which I have suffered for too long, but I was not alone in my ordeal. My Cousin Jack, also a renegade, was my most fervent friend and ally, and so I leave him now, etc. etc. etc. . . ."

I think one can truly say that we know how lonely some people are by those they name to be their closest and dearest.

Jervis Spyker

* *
 *

He was my uncle, and well-beloved by all, an original, too; you would have to say that of him, for he courted well into his seventieth year the same woman, twenty years older than himself, Mavis Spinner, the daughter of a physician, who inherited much wealth. She inhabited "rooms" in the Queensbury Hotel, and all her long life of clipping coupons, and savoring imported cherry-centered chocolate bonbons, Uncle Jervis was there with her to be with her, a most constant and attentive courtier, in that avoirdupoid court.

Uncle Jervis was only discouraged the year Governor Thomas E. Dewey died of the apoplexy, when Mavis was stricken in a most untimely way of a similar complaint, and lingered awhile before passing over into most awful putrefaction, and then he was sorely heartbroken, grieved a lot, and died.

Some people said, "Mavis died of a broken heart for the little Governor, and Jervis died of a broken heart for Mavis."

He was one of God's better men: constant, and true, and the only member of our family with a connection to the sea, and its crafts, from which springs forth our name.

Spyker, you understand, is a contraction, like a cramp in the fist, of the older Frisian and English word for a forward sail, the so-called Spinnaker which coils against our tongues as a piece of maritime nomenclature even to this day. So we Spykers were originally sailmakers, and then raftsmen, and barge captains, and so the name: Uncle Jervis kept the lock at Smith's Basin, and lived nearby in a small white house.

He had two unusual expressions: "Bejesus as I am seen in the shower" and "Get the fleas out of your ears," and used them, alternately, to express extreme surprise. He also had a way of expressing chagrin: He would say, "O Gawd," referring to the Almighty as if his word for the idea rhymed with an implement of steel used in ancient warfare.

Uncle Jervis stood well over six feet, and wore his hair cropped short, with a bald spot in the center that was reminiscent of a tonsure.

They say that as a younger man he loved men and women equally, and then he met Mavis and fell in love and was faithful to her more than fifty years.

What was her singular attraction? Some people said my uncle was trying to climb and better himself with her fortune, but when a man of seventy courts a woman of ninety with the ardor of a movie swain it must be he has thrown aside all such ordinary callous calculation.

In the Log Book he kept at his Lock there is only one entry concerning Mavis: "She is deliciously fat. I imagine her fat is as yellow as a chicken's and as oozy thick as the finest white honeycomb tripes. She bolsters me. She supports my spirits. Afterwards I am uplifted on this warm soft mattress of her love-fat."

John Spyker The Redhead

* *
 *

Some people think he is me, as we bear the same surnames and family names, and are distant cousins, of a sort; so, to distinguish us, the townspeople have appended to his name "The Redhead."

He is really more like strawberry blond, whereas I am now mostly all grey on top, and was once a brunet.

We used to be friends.

I never got along with his wife.

She used to call me homo. She said she was just teasing. I didn't think it was so funny.

He has worked for the Niagara Mohawk as long as I can remember, and is now in charge of all the substations and their maintenance between here and North Elba.

He's a decent responsible sort, and I never heard a word of scandal that clung to his name. But he was once confined to the Mental Health Center for about a week because he was feeling "sorta down" and it turned out he had tried out suicide, and failed.

One other thing: his only brother, Sal, lives in Elmira and, now that the wife is dead, he visits every weekend and the two walk hand in hand in identical camel's-hair topcoats along the tow-path.

I think they're queer together, two brothers, but I would never tell anybody that. It's his business, I say.

Their business. When you've lived in Fort Edward as long as John Spyker and myself you can do anything and people just say, "Oh, you know John. That's his way . . . is all. . . ."

A Queer But Sweet Story
From Aldrich Spinker

* *
 *

The following was related to me by my half-cousin, Aldrich Spinker.

He was in Italy, shortly after the war ended, to recommence the family business.

Aldrich & Sons are importers of licorice and pignoli nuts, and some other spices, for the Greater Albanian area.

He had gone to a small town in the region known as Romagna to inquire after one of his former suppliers. Had he survived Mussolini and the Partisans?

The man was fine, good as new. They made a little business together.

At the local *albergo* where he was staying a certain Signora Altrichetti called on the telephone to ask if he, Mr. Spinker, had yet arrived and how long he might be staying on.

The clerk, Zimmer, said he thought Spinker's caller was an Australian, or a South African woman.

Aldrich was puzzled, and surprised. He had never been to Italy before the war; his mother did most of the buying in those days; and he had told nobody of his travel plans, knew of nobody in this little city, aside from his supplier, and he not overly well.

He got on the phone and asked the Altrichetti woman if she spoke English.

"Of course, John."

"Do I know you?" he asked, recognizing a certain homey flatness of accent.

"By Gawd," she exclaimed, "you must remember me. I was the former Phoebe Bight when you and I were in knickers. We went to school together. . . ."

"Not Boom Boom?" Aldrich declared, finding himself blushing.

"The very same . . . just the same as you are Black Aldrich. . . ."

They had a laugh over the fact that A always had black teeth from his mother's licorice.

They also joked about the clerk thinking she might be an Aussie, and made a date to have cocktails that evening at Phoebe's villa.

Such fellow feeling is likely to occur whenever two County classmates bump heads in an exotic place.

It's a wonder they didn't bewail the fate of old Jane MacCrea.

It seems Boom Boom Phoebe had recently widowed herself of a wealthy Italian landowner who sheltered her throughout the whole war on the island of Elba, and she was still very devoted to his memory.

Phoebe Bight was also still pretty, in her way, Aldrich said, but fat; and he confided to me that he was granted every hospitality and wound up spending the night, losing himself, as it were, in her delicious pleasures.

In the morning when he was dressing Cousin Aldrich proposed to Phoebe, somewhat perfunctorily, that she consider coming back to visit the old homestead for a time.

"Not on your life," she said. "This is my true home nowadays. . . ."

I asked Aldrich what happened next.

"She told me her *casa* was my *casa* whenever, and I left and never saw her again. . . ."

"Sounds like a dream come true," I said.

Aldrich frowned: "More like a lesson in the geography of love. . . ."

I asked him to explain what he meant.

"Where she was available I was not," Aldrich said, "and likewise vice versa. So we were at what you might call catty-corners with our affections. . . ."

"And do you know what's happening to her these days?"

Aldrich winced, and reminded me he had retired from the spice importing business over a decade ago.

He said, "She never writes. I don't think she would like to remember past a certain point. She has one son in sardines is all I know."

Colly Degnan

* *
*

This old Irishwoman used to clean for Ma. She died rich. Her son went to RPI. She had a favorite expression about the difference between making *tea* and making *water*. Otherwise she was not profane. I once overheard her telling Ma how Degnan had never seen her without her shift, yet they had produced a son, and a daughter, both normal children.

She told me once there were "so many Spinkers, Spuyckers, Spookers, and Spickers in the County and all related" she "had a mind to think a quarrel among the relations somewhere had festered and the results were pretty awesome to contemplate."

I often reflect on how she managed to speak more eloquently than most people can write down their thoughts, and I assume it had to do with her low estate, and that she considered it urgent in speaking to her "betters" that she be easily "apprehended."

Ramsey

* *
 *

All we know of this man (or woman) who called himself (herself) Ramsey are found in two fragments of verse scribbled on the walls of the old opera house in Fort Edward before it was painted over to become a wholesale butchering supplier:

> The weather cooking across the Lake
> brought me here to a party of angry spooks . . .
>
> ***
>
> Like blisters on the moon
> the green and yellow leaves
> have come and gone. All is
> darkening. All

The break that occurs here is really a blur of Pentel blue, smudge or smear, suggesting that while both were obviously written by the same hand the second was the more rapidly composed.

The Lake could be either Summit, Cossayuna, George, Schroon, Loon, or Gawd knows what, but the classical lines remind me a little of some I encountered once in a gay bar in Fort Ti:

> *Animula Vagula, Blandula Fagula*

William Bronk,
Poet & Lumberman
* *
*

Here is a curious case of virtue being its own best
reward, I suppose. This fellow Bronk has garnered
fame by avoiding people, and he has achieved a reputation by shunning the public eye. The person never
lived who did not love to be admired, I have always
been told, not to mention adored, but Bronk is a
strange crabby sort of man, and he prefers to be
respected, and feared.

I have seen him only once or twice on Main Street
during his evening promenades and would assert
there was nothing wooden about his posture: a man in
his late fifties of better than average height with
strong features, a large nose, high forehead, glasses,
this wide sensual mouth, and a good smile. He is said
to be not overly fond of most people and gives them
only short and cursory notice with his eyes, but has an
eye for all children, a ready greeting, and easy manner for them and their pets.

I know not much else worth saying of this pre-
eminent member of our Washington County family
except to report that his two older sisters have married and moved away long years past; he, being a
bachelor, lives for part of every year with his elderly
mother, much as I once used to do with my own
mamma.

Bronk's poetry is becoming highly prized by certain of his contemporaries, and he has been reviewed in our leading journals, and papers. The editions are costly and small, and he does not require any income from his art, though he also does not, in his words, "live in a hogan under a hovering sky."

I have done some cursory research into the career: after an expensive education at Dartmouth and Harvard, and service during the war with the Coastal Artillery in Bermuda, this fellow inherited a large interest in his father's lumberyard, along with an uncle.

Bronk was father to nobody and husband never at all, so his needs are not great: a fine old yellow house and garden on Pearl Street is his domain; and he writes of it, often and well; he grows herbs, and lives prudently, but was always a poetaster, as well as poet, with a worldwide correspondence among other wordsmiths, and a deeply resonant reading voice to regale his friends when they visit. He is still, I believe, a stout benefactor to all the local enterprises of art and culture: the renowned Hyde Museum in the Falls; the summer opera series at Lake George; the chamber music concerts of the De Biases; and his other great recreation is walking, particularly along the overgrown and disused towpaths of the old Feeder Canal.

Bronk seems to have made many young friends during this lifetime, and numerous good acquaintances of an international repute.

Though I have never spoken to the man face to face I have read and enjoyed many of his poems in magazines and books. They are admirable, when not merely competent, and inspired by a stunning regionalist rectitude, I think, a good eye, and a keen ear which, however, sometimes lacks finesse; for he is apt to advertise his postal zone number (which is 12839) in a poem for "the happy few" who read him, or berate his own gonads for the troubles they sometimes inspire in him, and his language can be occasionally profane, not to mention caustic, and offensive to one of some sensibility, such as the former poet, Richard Eberhart.

He is said to be an excellent cook and baker of breads and a fine host, with an account at Sherry-Lehmann's in metropolitan Gotham that supplies him liberally with spirits of every conceivable variety, and a palate that inclines to the odd, and the peculiar, such as our local spring morels in dill sauce, the young milkweeds boiled in vinegar, and a dish he calls "brains and balls" which is just what it would seem to be.

This prodigious walker is also an accomplished gossip, as are most of my neighbors, and a generous and kindly householder.

He is said to be even more gentle toward his mother than I was toward my own in her old age, and he has been known to befriend stray animals.

He has a comely girlfriend for whom I once lusted.

It may seem odd to you that in a neighborhood as modest as our Sandy Hill vicinity two such eminent belletrists as Bronk and myself have never struck up a speaking acquaintanceship, but that is part of the character of our little place in the sun. I doubt if Bronk even knows of my existence. The snob, he is much too self-absorbed; and the Spuycker name, though celebrated locally, is not commonly associated with things of cultural variety.

May I also remind the reader that the renowned

Frederick Goddard Tuckerman and Emily Dickinson both lived in Amherst, Massachusetts, during the last century only a few blocks apart, and though both were among the pre-eminent poets of their era we have no records extant of any intercourse whatsoever between the author of "I heard a fly buzz when I died" and the author of "Crickets."

Besides, I am even more shy and retiring about my work than Bronk who has given public readings at the Crandall Library, and elsewhere in the vicinity.

But if we were friends I wonder what we might have to say to one another beyond the little admiring things a friend is apt to put out, for the sake of civility. That two such as ourselves, from among the County's leading families, should have chosen the bramble path of poetry as their life's calling, unacknowledged, and largely unrewarded for our labors, does not necessarily make for a rivalry, but it is also not, perforce, the route to any intimate chumship.

Bronk's ancestors were outlanders, like my own. He is said to be the last living male descendant of a certain Captain Broenk, a Dutchman, who arrived with his own shipload of persons and goods in New Amsterdam in the decade of Peter Stuyvesant.

The family later established their patroonship in the vicinity of Selkirk in Green County, and New Baltimore, until the Senior Bronk, Wm's father, a man "lacking in any recreation save for the making of money," and an importer of Italian laborers for his construction business, repaired himself with his young wife further north to our County to establish himself in coal, construction, lumberyards.

The Bronx is named after this same family (that borough being among their earliest domains for farming), and there are distant cousins everywhere in the State, including another Bill Bronk in the Falls who is, I believe, a doctor of sorts.

The mother in her prime was a Republican State Committeewoman, and the father also may have owned a bank and was County Welfare Commissioner.

All else that I know or have conjectured from hearsay should remain hearsay, for I do not know these things as fact, or with any intimacy. Not being the intimate of Bronk, except from my very great hailing distance, I find him admirable, I suppose, if I would not also say I admired him, or was desirous of making his further acquaintance. He may be that genuine poet of our New York stock we are all so desirous of acknowledging; and, then again, I might be "Martin Van Buren's left testicle," as we used to say in the County, or "the nephew of Rameau."

Epilog
A Poem Composed By My Father,
Who Also Called Himself John Sp(u)y(c)ker,
Written When He Was My Age,
For His Fellow Masons And
Odd Fellows Of All Ages

Here's to the urge that brings on the dirge:
Here's to the titty, the ditty, the dirge.
And here's to the urge
that brings on your dirge,
the titty the dirge,
the ditty the dirge:
the titty the ditty the dirge.
for that urge is a purge
of our life force's surge
and the pity's the ditty
if life is so shitty
the worst pain of all is that urge,
Amen,
and the worst pain of all is that urge,
and finally there's just *your* dirge. . . .

This concludes my LITTLE LIVES. I contemplate a second volume on the history of the Sp(u)y(c)ker clan.

The author would like to thank Mrs. J. B. Vanderwerker, whose reminiscences of the County appeared some years back in the *Saratogian,* and in one privately printed pamphlet.

215